The Good Wine

Also Available by Amy Schisler

Novels
A Place to Call Home
Picture Me
Whispering Vines
Summer's Squall
The Devil's Fortune

Chincoteague Island Trilogy
Island of Miracles
Island of Promise
Island of Hope

Buffalo River Series
Desert Fire, Mountain Rain

Children's Books
Crabbing With Granddad
The Greatest Gift

Spiritual Books
Stations of the Cross Meditations for Moms (with Anne Kennedy, Susan Anthony, Chandi Owen, and Wendy Clark)
A Devotional Alphabet

The Good Wine

By Amy Schisler

ISBN-13: 978-1-7346907-4-3

Published by:
Chesapeake Sunrise Publishing
Amy Schisler
Bozman, MD
2021

To my dear readers,

It's hard to believe that *The Good Wine* is my tenth novel. For fourteen years, I have written full time, spending my days inside worlds of my own imagination where characters collide, faith is deepened, love is discovered, and dreams come true.

It is within this world that I have met people who have changed me in some way, who have allowed my own faith to be strengthened, and who have challenged me to reach deeper, try harder, and write better. Every word, every scene, every story comes from my heart but is inspired by those I meet and by those I aspire to be, in real life and in my imagination.

When I wrote *Whispering Vines* six years ago, Marta went from a collection of words on my computer screen to a real person with a past and a story. I knew when I first met her, wandering through the fictional fields of Belle Uve with Alex, that I had to write about her and tell the story she had to tell, but I was not ready. It took these past six years, and the creation of other characters, for me to truly know who Marta is and how best to share her story with you. It had to be something special, something that incorporated my faith, my writing, my love of both Italy and my home state of Maryland, and a few characters from past books (not just the obvious ones). I wanted Marta's feelings and her story to be recognizable to people of all ages. I hope that you will find this to be the case.

Ten novels and fourteen years of writing—in some ways, it's a very short time, but all those years are worth celebrating, and there are many people with whom I'd like to celebrate this achievement. I could not write these books or continue on this path without the love and encouragement of my tribe. Anne, Tammi, Dotty, Chandi, Ronnie, Marian, Victoria, Michelle, Laurie, Donna, Jeanne, and Susan, you are my sounding board, my literary team, my publicists, my inspiration, and my best friends. It sounds like I should be paying you! But you all pay me every day with your love and support. You help me with everything from story ideas to beta reading, by taking me to places that inspire me, and by praying for and with me. So much of my writing would not exist without you. I love you all so much and pray for you daily.

Cheryl, Cindy, Debbie, one a lifelong friend, one a college roommate, and one a fellow elementary school mom, you all have been a part of my life for so many years. I cannot imagine doing this without you. Thank you for encouraging me, for sharing my books with others, and for being my dear, dear friends. I hope you know how much I love you all.

Mom, Dad, Mom Schisler, Lisa, and Chrissy, my loving family, cheerleaders, promotors, supporters, traveling partners, and prayer warriors, thank you for being there for me, for loving me, and for being the important people you are in my life. Ken, Rebecca, Katie Ann, and Morgan, thank you for being the light in my life, the smile on my face, and the joy I find in each day. I love all of you.

Thank you, God, for all these years of doing what I love and for bringing all these people, real and fictional, into my life.

If you're ever in Florence, be sure to ask for Antonella Fantoni. You can ask for her by name through Vince at PlanitItaly.com. You won't regret it. She's an amazing guide, and I'm so happy to now call her my friend.

To those I have mentioned, to my friends, my readers, and all who have touched my life in some way, I say, life is short; drink the Good Wine.

Saluti!

To all those who love. To those who loved and lost, and to those who loved, lost, and then found. May you always drink the good wine.

"I have found the paradox, that if you love until it hurts, there can be no more hurt, only more love."

- Daphne Rae
Often attributed to St. Mother Teresa of Calcutta

Chapter One

1 June 1983

I think I'm too old to begin, Dear Diary, or with some other such opening. I've never journaled before, but Zia Isabella insists that I journal while I am here in America this summer, the last summer of my freedom, as my university flat mates were calling it before I told them all goodbye in Florence and boarded my plane to Baltimore.

Graduation was just a week ago, and here I am, lying on what is now my bed at Zia Isabella's house in Little Italy. I only met my aunt once when I was a child, but she has always been a part of my life, my papà's younger sister who mysteriously fled Italy during The War. I am here spending my summer abroad, as they say, visiting art museums, taking pictures, perfecting my English—this is why I write in English in this journal and not in Italian—and learning about the American states. In the fall, after I return, I will marry Piero, the love of my life, and he will take me away from our family's vineyard where I have spent almost my entire boring life, listening to my papà always searching for the way to make ~~un buon vino~~, a good wine—il primo wine, no, the best wine. Sometimes I feel all that matters in the world is wine, and now Piero is working on il vineyard, too, but he does not care about wine. He wants to teach, and I want to work in museum. This is what I count days for, to marry Piero and live away from Belle Uve. I am tired of living on a vineyard and yearn to stay in Firenze. I hated to say goodbye to my flat mates and our adventures at university, and I can't wait to be back in city, this time with Piero.

He wrote to me as soon as I left Italy, maybe before. His letter arrived today, so he must have sent it before or on the day I left for it to arrive so soon. That makes me as happy as a schoolgirl, which I am only a few days past being.

This afternoon, with screen door slamming behind me as I entered la casa, I heard Zia Isabella's still accented voice calling to me with exciting, of exciting? in exciting? Allora...

She called, "Marta, you have a letter! Es from Piero."

I followed the sound of her voice to the kitchen, the bag with my camera bouncing against my hip. Zia

Isabella seems always to be in the kitchen. She once told me that cooking makes her feel like she is back in Italy. Why she has never returned to Italy, I do not know. Nobody does. The War was over many years ago, and still, she will not return. She says she is American now even if she will always be Italian in her heart.

When I walked through the doorway, my beautiful zia, wearing an apron and her hair tied in a neat chignon behind her head, was waving an envelope in air. She was smiling, and her eyes twinkled. Even nearing fifty, she is beautiful with her raven hair and olive skin. I hope that I have those same genes and look that good when I am old. Not that Zia Isabella could ever be old, but allora, she is almost fifty.

"Already?" I asked her in Italian. Even though I promised Zia Isabella I would only speak English, when I am excited, that is not so easy to remember. It feels like weeks since I have seen Piero, and my hand trembled as I tore open the letter. The letter began,

"My dearest Marta, How I miss you. The sun does not shine the same, and the birdsong is filled with melancholy notes."

My heart elevarsi when I read the rest of the letter, and by the time I was finished, tears streamed down my face. I could not help it. I missed him so much.

Zia Isabella asked if everything was all right. I told her that everything is bene, that Piero misses me but is working hard.

Before I left, Papà told me that he was very pleased with the vines so far and that he was just as pleased with Piero's hard work. The spring was bene to us, not too much or too little rain, and Piero is happy about spending the summer working on the vineyard with Papà. He hopes to have enough money, by the time I return, to buy us a house in Firenze. I will miss Mamma e Papà, but I want so much to live in the city and work at Il Uffizi while Piero teaches at university.

When I tried to smile through my tears, Zia Isabella grabbed my hand and squeezed it. She asked if I miss Piero very much, and I do, but I am so happy to be here this summer. I am very happy to have this summer with the aunt I have always wanted to know better, who spoiled me from afar, and whose voice I only heard on Christmas and on mio birthday, sounding distant amidst the crackling on the phone.

As I wrote before, Zia Isabella fled Italy during the war, and to this day, she has never told a soul why or what happened. She and Zio Roberto disappeared during the night, were married in secret, and made their way to America. Nobody knows how they managed it, but here they are, and here they stay. Neither has ever gone back home even for a short visit, and as sad as that is, it's also the most romantic story I know. I pray that Piero and I have some kind of romantic story to tell someday. Meeting in study group during exam time does not sound very romantic, but we will have a lifetime to make romance.

We are very different. He loves to teach about mathematics, and I love to study art and take photographs, but we are in love, and this is all that matters.

Today, before I even knew about the letter, I visited the Baltimore Art Museum. There are so many beautiful works of art that I did not know had been brought to America. I cannot wait to go to Washington this weekend. Zio Roberto says I will be amazed by the National Gallery of Art though he warned that it is no Uffizi.

"No place is like Il Uffizi," Zia Isabella likes to say, always with a warm smile. She keeps telling me how proud she is that I will work at Il Uffizi. It is the crown jewel of Firenze where, if I want to, I can gaze daily at Botticelli's Birth of Venus or da Vinci's The Annunciation. I am in awe each time I walk through the doors, and I cannot believe I will be working there by end of summer.

Allora, first, I want to enjoy this summer with Zia Isabella and Zio Roberto. When I return home, I *will have a job and soon a husband. For now, I am still Marta Abelli, free to see the world, and so far I am in love with America. Almost as much as I am in love with Piero.*

Little Italy, Baltimore, June 2019

Marta stood on the docks and looked out over the water. So much had changed in the past thirty-six years, yet so much remained the same. The USS Constellation was still there, rocking on the waves produced by the passing boats. She remembered touring the ship with her Uncle Roberto. Beyond the warship, along the red-brick-paved dock, she recognized the colorful landscape of blue-windowed buildings, red umbrella-covered restaurants, and green slatted roofs over the Inner Harbor shops. The buildings were the same, but many of the names and types of shops had changed. She snapped a few pictures and sighed, recalling the times she had spent on these same docks taking pictures of the boats, the passersby, the gulls overhead, and of…

She shook away the thought and looked around. From what she had seen on her ride from the airport, much of the city outside of the central downtown had lost its allure, no longer holding the charm that was once Charm City, but that was normal of any industrialized city, she supposed. The same could be said of Florence or Rome. According to what she read online, Baltimore's Little Italy was still a vibrant jewel in the city's crown with its restaurants, pastry shops, and Italian markets that reminded her of home. She could remember visiting them that summer, listening to the beautiful cadence of her native tongue from the few who still spoke the language. Too many years had gone by, and Marta wondered if there was more Spanish spoken in the city than Italian. She wondered how the Polish and Ukrainian neighborhoods had fared. They were already getting smaller, crowded out by other groups, when she was here those many years ago.

She walked along the bricks, listening to gulls calling out overhead, often drowned out by the laughter of children, the droning of motors, and the blowing whistles of the incoming water traffic. She stopped to watch a family toss breadcrumbs into the harbor; a little girl squealed in delight as a duck scooped a piece of crust into its bill. The scene took her back to a summer day in June, another walk along the dock, the tossing of bread to the ducks, and the warm feeling of a strong hand holding hers.

Marta smiled at the memory. It was a long time ago, but the memory was a cherished one—a stolen afternoon, a secret rendezvous, the thrill of something forbidden and unknown. She took a long, deep breath and pictured his eyes, so warm and caring, the color of the sea she traveled to on holiday so many times—the rich, blue-green hue of the Mediterranean on a hot July day. She remembered once when Nicola was just three, running in the sand along the sea that reminded her of…

She stopped and shook her head. Feeling the same guilt now that she had felt then, she chastised herself for allowing Nicola, her son by Piero, to be part of the memory of that time in her life, a time that was shadowed in secrecy.

She looked down at the bare finger on her left hand and felt another stab of guilt. Just before she left home at the urging of her dearest friend, Antonella, she had slipped the ring from her hand and placed it gently in her jewelry box. Now, she wondered if that had been wrong, to remove the symbol of her marriage as though she was removing Piero from her life.

She sighed heavily. Must she still carry so much guilt? She had done nothing wrong, not now and not back then. Allora, almost nothing. In the end, she had not broken her promise and had returned home as she was supposed to. She had gone back to Italy at the end of the summer, married Piero, and after much pain and heartache, they had finally had Nicola, the light of her life who now ran their family vineyard, Belle Uve. She had put all thoughts of that summer behind her, concentrating on her life as a wife and mother, forsaking childish fantasies of things that were never meant to be. She'd had a good life, a happy life, and had lost Piero too soon to a sudden heart attack that had taken him away from her and from their son, now grown and married, a father himself.

But her daughter-in-law, dear, sweet Alexandra, had brought the memories back, forcing them through the wall she'd so carefully constructed, like a break in a damn. Ever since the night she first met her son's future wife, when Alexandra was nothing more than an American stranger thrust upon them, she had been thinking about Zia Isabella, about the house in Little Italy, and the man she'd left behind.

Was she here to finally say goodbye to those memories? To put the ghosts of a past life to rest? Or to discover what possibilities lie ahead? Those were questions Marta was not certain she was ready to answer.

Marta slipped off her traveling shoes just inside the front door and left them in the lipped, rubber mat that she thought might be the same one that had been there in 1983. She latched the screen door and kept open the storm door to welcome the breeze, then hung her purse in the closet, just as Zia Isabella used to do. She hadn't opened the house completely in her haste to see the downtown before it got dark, and it was stuffy, smelling faintly of mildew and dust and the other smells that told the age of a house. The furniture was covered with sheets, and she coughed as she pulled them off, throwing dust particles, dead bugs, and who knew what else swirling into the air around her.

Alexandra had inherited the house from Marta's aunt, Isabella, always referred to by Alexandra as Signora unless they were talking of Isabella as a young woman, who referred to herself as Isa. The elderly woman had become a surrogate grandmother to young Alex who had been in college when she became Isa's caretaker. Isabella obviously saw in the quiet, shy girl the woman she would become, bestowing upon Alex not just the house but half of the family vineyard. Marta could easily see why Zia Isabella had been so taken with the young woman. Marta's son, Nicola, was smitten almost instantly though their road from strangers quarreling over how to run the vineyard to a head-over-heels in love couple was as rocky as the Amalfi coast. Still, Zia Isabella somehow knew that Alex and Nicola were meant to be together just as Marta knew from the moment she met Alex and saw her and Nicola sparring over their everyday routines.

Alexandra and Nicola had traveled to Baltimore after they were married with the intention of selling the house, but something made them hold onto it. Perhaps Alexandra thought they would come back from time to time, an opportunity for her to show their children what her life in America was like. Allora, with two children running the fields to pluck the grapes from the vines, one more ripening in utero, and a vast amount of grapes to tend, Alexandra and Nicola rarely left the vineyard.

Marta smiled as she pictured their faces when she asked if she could use the house for a few weeks.

"But Mamma, how will you manage alone?" Nicola had asked, his eyes filled with worry as though she was incapable of traveling alone.

She'd laughed. "The same way I manage my home, Nicola, and my life in Firenze. What do you think I am? A child who needs looking after?"

As though to prove a point, little Carlos ran into the room, his hands covered with chocolate. "Nonna! Chocolate!"

"I see," Marta said with a laugh. "Be careful. You're going to get it everywhere."

While Alex tended to Carlos, Marta explained her plans to Nicola. She would be gone a few weeks, maybe a month, working on a deal between the Uffizi, where she had gone back to work after Piero's death, and the National Gallery of Art in Washington.

"The museum would pay for a hotel," she told Nicola. "But why should they when you have a house there?"

She explained that the negotiations would take a week or so, and once the decisions had been made about which works of art would be temporarily exchanged, and the ink on the deal was dry, Marta would have time to reconnect with her memories of Zia Isabella and Zio Roberto, the neighborhood, and perhaps an old friend or two…

Nicola raised a brow and inquired as to what friends she had kept in America all these years, but Marta waved him off.

"You are familiar with social media, no? I have ways of connecting with old friends."

The truth was, she had not reconnected with old friends, but she had tried stalking a person or two. Her once dear friend, Angela, was nowhere to be found which was terribly disappointing. Her friend, Paul, looked to be happily married, but he almost never posted, and she learned very little about his life. And there was another person in particular she had looked for, had hoped to find living a happy life—or perhaps had dreaded seeing the details of his happy life—but he could not be found. Had he moved? Did he continue to live a secret life of intrigue? Was he…? No, that was a question she refused to ask.

Once Nicola realized she had her mind made up, he relented. And here she was, standing in the little living room of the quiet house surrounded by ghosts. She couldn't even walk into the cheery, yellow kitchen without expecting to see her aunt. She needed to get used to the feel of the empty house, but her memories were so strong that they pulled her into the past at every turn. Her mind played the sound of dishes clinking, and her nose still detected the scent of her uncle's cigars mingled with the baking of bread or Italian pastries. Zio Roberto liked to smoke just one cigar each evening after work, and the memory and smell were not unpleasant.

And from the house down the street, with the grey bricks and white stoop, the eyes that once again had begun haunting her dreams still watched her as she walked by…

3 June 1983

I imagined that the air in America would be filled with the sweet fragrance of wisteria blossoms like it was on the vineyard. I knew the city would be very different from the vineyard, different even from Verona or Firenze, but I didn't think it would be all brick, house connected to house, no trees, and a closeness that feels stifling. Cars speed by with smelly scarico pouring from the tail pipes, and ~~rifiuti~~ rubbish blows down the street, carried by wind like leaves in fall.

I keep trying to take photographs, but there is not much to see in the small corner of city I am allowed to be in. It is cleaner and ben tenuto, but there is not anything to capture with my camera. My artist's eye has not spied a single interesting thing so far.

Today, when I was walking, trying desperately to find a good photo opportunity, I stopped and closed my eyes and tried to imagine the smell of grapes on the vine, but instead, I coughed, choking on fumi di scarico and the smell of rotting rubbish coming from the cans at the curbside.

I heard a voice call out, "Are you going to stand there like that all day or just until you breathe in enough (he used a parolaccia – a word I will not repeat) to give you cancer?"

Startled, I opened my eyes and turned toward the house where I saw a boy standing on what I think passes for a portico but was not more than a few steps with a tendalino overhead. I felt heat rise to my face and wanted to hide like a little girl caught doing something naughty.

I answered in forced English, feeling nervous but not wanting him to know it. I asked, "Is it a crime in America to enjoy the smell of the outdoors?"

The boy shrugged his shoulders and said there wasn't much to enjoy about it unless you knew how to pick out the good smells from bad. He said that after a while, your nose can identify the good stuff, like when someone is baking bread or making marinara. He said, "Those smells will make you want to stand outside someone's window all afternoon." His look led me to believe that he had done just that on many afternoons.

Then, the boy bounded down the steps like an Olympian and came toward me, and I realized he was not a boy at all. He was almost as tall as Piero, and he had a light shadow on his chin. He came nearer, and I was struck by his boldness.

He stuck out his hand and said, "I'm Paul. And you are?"

I recalled this strange custom of shaking hands rather than kissing each cheek, and I took his hand. He shook mine heartily.

I was still nervous and stuttered, "My papà is Pablo, like you. I am Marta. Marta Abelli."

That boy! He said, "Well, Marta Marta. I'm just Paul. I've never met anyone with two first names that are the same. And only my nonna calls me Pablo."

I wondered, how dare he make fun of me? I cocked my head and narrowed my eyes, and he laughed.

He told me he was just kidding and asked, "So, Marta, are you from Italy? My guess is yes, based on your accent and the fact that you're staying with Signor and Signora Fonticelli."

His accent sounded plainly American, unlike Zia Isabella and her friends who all sounded very Italian even after all these years. I wondered if this Paul lived in the house with the tiny portico, or if he was visiting, or perhaps doing work of some sort, but he wasn't dressed for lavoro. He wore navy shorts and a white t-shirt.

I answered him, "Si. I am visiting mi Zia Isabella." I watched his eyes as he gave a quick nod.

He told me that Zia Isabella is friends with his mamma but that he didn't know she had a niece.

I began to ramble. I told him that Zia Isabella is mi papà's sister, that she left Italy many, many years ago, long before Papà and Mamma met, and that I did not know her well except through letters and a few phone calls though I had visited her here once when I was very little.

"It must be strange, then, to be living there and not really know each other," he said, and I didn't know what to say. I have never felt that Zia Isabella was a stranger.

I told him, "Allora, no. Zia Isabella has always been a part of my life. I have been told that we look alike."

As his eyes roved over me, I felt exposed and ~~cosciente~~ conscious, self-conscious, I think. He looked at me from head to toe then squinted as though to see me better, and said, "I guess so. I mean, you're prettier than she is."

I felt my cheeks grow warm and looked at my feet, and he apologized.

I smiled and looked up at him, giving him my own assessment. I decided that he was not a man after all. My first assumption was correct. He was younger than me by a few years, just a year or two shy of being a man, but he was tall and had a confidence about him that made him seem older. I told him it was okay and thanked him, but I could not remember the right word I wanted to use. I stammered and strung words together that must not have made sense before asking him for help.

"You mean, compliment?" he asked.

I said sí, that was the word I was looking for, but I suddenly felt as though I was saying too much. I did not know this boy.

Then Paul, that confident, forward, almost-man said, "You know, I could show you around, make sure you know your way and all. I know which bakery has the best cannoli and where it's safest to walk." He then pointed to the camera around my neck and asked if I was a photographer.

I told him that I hope to be someday.

Then, a sudden movement caught my attention, and I turned back toward Paul's casa. A slightly older version of Paul had stepped onto the portico, but there was no smile, no welcoming wave or attempt to move closer. Something about the man—for this was indeed a man—something about his gaze caught me unawares, and I felt my breath catch in my throat. He stood, staring intently at me, his arms crossed, a frown darkening his features. They looked alike, he and Paul, but where Paul exuded friendliness and openness, this man was shrouded with such fierce coldness it made me shiver. He broke eyes with me, and I was grateful, and he looked at Paul.

His voice was scolding when he said, "Mamma asked you to go to the market. Did you forget?"

Paul answered, "No, I didn't forget, Dominic. I was just leaving." Paul turned back to me, and I forced myself to turn my gaze from this Dominic.

Paul asked me if I wanted to go to the market with him. His eyes sparkled with hope, but I shook my head and felt sorry for the disappointment that replaced the hope.

I told him that I should be going. Zia Isabella did not expect me to be gone so long.

I watched Paul walk away and knew that I, too, was being watched. I gathered a breath and turned slowly toward the house, but nobody was there. I blinked and wondered where he had gone. Why did I still feel his eyes upon me? A shiver ran down my back as I began slowly walking away. As soon as I was far enough away from the house, I picked up my pace and ran back to Zia Isabella's. Something about Dominic, I'm not sure what, makes me uncomfortable, and I hope not to see him again.

Marta told herself that she would spend her first night back in America getting reacquainted with the house. After she texted both Nicola and her best friend, Antonella, to tell them that she had survived her first day there, she moved her clothes into the dresser that had once belonged to her aunt and put fresh sheets on the double bed. She went down the hall and sat on the twin bed in the little guest room and recalled how it looked that summer with photographs stuck in the frame of the mirror and her makeup strewn across the dresser scarf. Lacy, yellow curtains had fluttered in front of an open window where white panels now hung. A light puff of air from the fan overhead stirred them, and Marta smiled. Zia Isabella never liked the air conditioning and rarely turned it on. Roberto used to tell her that they were too old to stand the heat, but her aunt would remind him that open windows were good enough for their family in Italy, and he would not argue with her after that. Then again, Zio Roberto rarely, if ever, argued with Zia Isabella. He was a quiet man who went to work each day and came home for dinner each night, who read the newspaper by the glow of the lamp and spoke as little as possible. His grey beard covered much of his face, and Marta knew from her father that much of the skin on his body was still scarred from the frostbite he suffered as a prisoner of war.

Marta made her way back down the stairs and stopped in the doorway to the kitchen. So many memories flooded back, and she found herself missing her aunt more than ever. There was no sauce cooking on the stove, no dough being rolled and cut into pasta, and no warm bread filling the kitchen with its tantalizing aroma. The yellow paint had faded from lemon rind to banana slices, and the wood floor no longer shined with a high varnish.

Nicola had arranged for food to be delivered and put away by their cleaning service, but nothing in the refrigerator appealed to her. None of it was what Zia Isabella would have been making had she been here.

Marta wondered if the little market on the corner was still open, and before she knew what she was doing, she found herself putting on her shoes and heading back out the door.

Most of the houses still looked the same. Some had been freshly painted, even over the bricks in some cases, but they still looked sturdy, standing one against the other with no space between. The neighborhood still smelled the same, the afternoon air heavily laden with the heady scents of garlic, oregano, and other spices — just as Paul had promised that day—and she found herself stopping to inhale, the smell carrying with it memories that flooded her senses as much as the spices did.

She closed her eyes, letting the smells fill her. She didn't need to open her eyes to know where she had stopped, but she did open them and gazed at the familiar building. The grey house with the tiny front porch looked just the same. The awning over the porch was green now instead of white, but nothing else had changed. Marta blinked as she recalled the first time she saw him, how he had frightened her, how his intense stare and crossed arms appeared so unwelcoming. How much there was that she did not know, did not understand, at that moment. How much she came to know in her short time in America, more knowledge and emotion than a young woman possibly could have handled. But handle it she did, as best she could knowing that their worlds would never be one.

The slamming of a screen door on a house nearby startled her and brought her back from the chapters she had left behind in the book she thought she had closed. She couldn't help but wonder if his family still lived there. Would whomever occupied the little house know of him, of where he went, where he was now? She closed her eyes and took in a long, meditative inhale and exhale, reminding herself that some books were best left on the shelf.

Chapter Two

5 June 1983

This afternoon, I heard voices downstairs and wondered who was here, so I tip-toed to the top of the staircase and peered down. I could see Zio Roberto's figure in the entryway and caught just a glimpse of a pair of skinny, bare legs opposite Zio Roberto in the doorway. My zio's frame turned a bit, and he called up the stairs to me, saying, "Marta, a young man is here to see you."

I was wearing a t-shirt, a pair of blue running shorts, and white canvas shoes that I found at the shopping mall. I think I looked very American with my new clothes and my long hair brushed straight and pulled into a sleek tail at the back of my head. I made my way slowly down the steps and smiled at Paul.

He said, "Hi, Marta. I came to give you that tour I promised."

Zio Roberto looked at me with wide eyes. I introduced Paul as someone who lived down the street, but I did not know his mother's name, and I knew that would matter.

Paul reached out his hand and said, "I'm Paul D'Angelo, Rosa's son."

Zio Roberto took his hand and said that he knew this and had seen Paul at church and around the neighborhood. He turned back to me and asked what this tour was.

I told him that I met Paul on my walk the other day, and he promised me a tour of the neighborhood. I bit my lip and waited for Zio Roberto to protest. He and Zia Isabella promised my parents that they would look out for me, and they barely let me out of their sight other than for short periods at a time or trips to a museum. I was sure he would say no.

Instead he asked, "How long will you be gone?" surprising me so much, I just stood and blinked at him, looking foolish I'm sure.

Paul spoke up right away, asking "What time would you like us to be back?" obviously no stranger to winning over one's parents. He quickly promised that we would not go far. He added, "I don't have a car."

I thought I detected a red sheen creep up his face, but his smile never faltered.

Zio Roberto put on a stern face when he answered, "Dinner is at six sharp. She needs to be back by then."

I stood there feeling like a child. I thought, aren't I old enough to be part of this conversation? Maybe I didn't even want to go.

Allora, but I did. I so wanted to meet other people my age, or near it anyway. And I found that, despite my own feelings of trepidation, I was curious about...

The deal was made, and Paul looked at me and asked, "Are you ready? Don't forget your camera."

I gave Zio Roberto a wide grin and ran up the stairs to retrieve my Canon F-1. When my feet hit the bottom step just seconds later, I leaned up to kiss mi zio gently on the cheek and said, "Grazie. I will be back in time for dinner."

I followed Paul out to the sidewalk, my mind buzzing with curiosity, and found myself disappointed when we began walking in the direction opposite of his house. We engaged in some idle chitchat about the neighborhood as Paul pointed out the bakery, an eatery he called a deli, and a new restaurant, Ciao Bella, that had just opened.

"It's very different," I told him, gazing at the buildings, so modern-looking in comparison to what I was used to. I said, "Despite its name , this does not look like Italy at all."

Paul laughed and explained, "It's called Little Italy because most of the immigrants who first lived here came from Italy, and now, everyone who lives here is an Italian-American." He said that there were also some people from Ireland and Germany and a number of Jewish immigrants living nearby, remnants of other large immigrant groups of the past, but by the 1920s, it was just Italians living on these few blocks. He told me that even more Italians came here after World War II.

I told him that was when Zio Roberto and Zia Isabella came and then remembered that I had told him that before.

Paul said, "Yeah, and my grandparents. They came here after the war." Then he asked me something I hadn't expected but should have. He said, "They're kind of old, aren't they? To be your aunt and uncle, I mean."

It is a question I am used to. I have often been asked that about my own father, so I answered the same way I always did.

"Sì. The war, it was not kind to Italy or its people. Some returned from war and started families. Some, like mi papa, took many years to find love and trust the world enough to have children. Some never found love or never had children."

He knew that my zio and zia did not have children and asked if it was hard for them.

I shook my head, feeling the conversation becoming too personal. These were things not discussed in my family, not ever. I never knew why Zia Isabella never had children or why she and Zio Roberto left Italy. I don't think my parents even know. Perhaps it had to do with Zio Roberto's imprisonment during the war, but that was something I never would have ventured to ask. Even if I did know, I would never talk about it to a total stranger. Instead, I turned on my camera, removed the lens cap, and started taking pictures to help me relax. Paul watched quietly.

After a few minutes, I put down the camera and asked, "Who was that man at your house the other day? Dominic, you called him."

"That's my brother." Paul said this as he kicked a rock, and it skidded across the sidewalk and into the street.

I said, "He seemed angry."

And Paul said, "He's always angry."

I looked sideways at Paul and asked, "At you?"

He said, "At me, my parents, the world." Paul shrugged. "But I think mostly at himself."

I thought about this and said, "I did not see him in church this morning. Is he angry with God?" I knew that I was the one asking questions too personal, but I could not resist.

"I guess you could say that," Paul said and then looked down at his watch. He said it was still early and asked if I wanted to visit the Shot Tower.

I didn't know what that was, so I said yes and found myself, a short walk later, staring up at a red brick tower that stretched high into the sky. Inside, I learned that the tower was over two-hundred feet tall and was a place where shot was made, lead pellets that were used by hunters to shoot ducks. Hot lead was dropped from the top of the tower into a box of water at the bottom of the tower, thus forming lead balls.

"What did you think?" Paul asked on our walk back.

I was honest and told him that I found it interesting inside, but the near-windowless, red brick building with an unadorned façade, was nothing like the towers back home. I told him that I don't think we have any museums of its kind in Italy and that it is nothing like the museum I will work in. I know that my photos will be interesting, and I told him this. I did not want him to think that I believed my country was better than his or that our buildings and museums were architecturally superior, though I did feel that way about many of them.

Paul asked, "You're going to work in a museum?"

I told him, sì, that I would be working at Il Uffizi in Florence and that I studied art at university.

Paul gave me a curious glance and asked, "How old are you anyway?"

I laughed and said, "You are not supposed to ask that." I pushed at his arm but smiled. I really did not mind. Paul has a way of putting one at ease, and I like him like I would like a younger brother if I had one.

He mumbled an apology, and I was quick to tell him it is fine. I told him that I am twenty-two, and he nodded and said, "Same as Dominic."

This surprised me, but I could not say why. It made sense that Paul's older brother would be close to my age, but his brooding looks and cross mannerisms made him seem even older.

I asked Paul how old he is, and he said he is seventeen and is going to university next year.

We stopped outside another red brick building, this one with a black tendalino like the ones on the shops in Italy. Along the tendalino were letters that read, Vaccaro's. Paul said, "This place has the best desserts in town. Come on."

I followed him inside and inhaled the familiar scents of sfogliatelle, pasticiotti, and napoleons. I closed my eyes, and for a moment, I was back in mamma's kitchen at Christmas time, when the house was filled with sweets. Though I knew that the dinner hour was approaching, I could not resist an éclair. Paul insisted on paying which was good since I had not thought to bring money.

There was little talking on the walk back as Paul and I savored our sweets. We were almost to Zia Isabella's when I heard Paul's name called out in a stern voice. Paul turned in the direction of the shout, his features hardening as Dominic walked toward us.

That accusing voice asked, "Where have you been? I had to take care of Nonno by myself. I could've used your help." I did not know what that meant, and Dominic looked at me and stiffened as though he had just noticed me standing next to his brother. I held a small bit of éclair in my hand and felt my heart quicken at the intensity of his gaze.

"I'm sorry," Dominic said more quietly. "We need Paul at home."

I nodded but found myself unable to answer as I gazed into eyes the color of the Mediterranean Sea.

"I'll see you later, Marta," I heard Paul say as he ran up the street toward his house, but I was frozen.

I held my breath as Dominic slowly raised his hand to my face and gently rubbed his thumb across my lower lip. "Chocolate," he said in a husky voice.

He took his thumb away, and I instinctively licked the place where he had touched my lip. His

Adam's apple bobbed, and a warm feeling rose from my stomach to my chest. I whispered, "Grazie."

We continued to stare at each other for moments, or perhaps days, until he slowly blinked his eyes and nodded. He turned and walked in the direction of his house, and I felt my knees go weak. I still am not sure what happened, but I feel that my world altered in a single breath.

On Sunday, Marta returned to the one place in America that had always felt as familiar to her as the vineyard itself. The facade of St. Leo the Great looked very much like many Italian churches. It boasted the traditional turret, bell tower, rose window, and decorative brickwork, but it was constructed with red brick rather than marble or stone. Inside, the resemblance to the churches she knew back home was undeniable. Designed by Baltimore architect, Francis Baldwin, and built by Italian immigrants, the church was constructed to be the social and spiritual focus of Baltimore Italians. By the number of congregants present, Marta could see that was still the case today.

The sanctuary was no Santa Maria Novella, her parish church back in Florence, but it was grand in its own right with plush red carpeted aisles and polished wooden pews that were surrounded by statues of saints along the walls and painted angels on the ceiling above.

The marble altar was encircled by saints carved into and painted on the walls with statues of angels, Mary, and St. John the Evangelist above the gold tabernacle. The beauty of the church with its celestial alcoves and immense pipe organ always drew Marta in and comforted her like the blanket she slept with as a child.

As she listened to the readings and the homily, she couldn't help but look around. Marta knew many intimate details about the church and was surprised at how easily those details came to mind after nearly forty years had passed since she learned them. The bell in the church's bell tower weighed over two-thousand pounds and was hoisted into place with a pulley tied to a team of horses. The pipe organ was the original, crafted by a German immigrant for the church in the 1800s. She knew that the paintings on the altar were done by two different artists and that the statues beneath the crucifix on the altar had been brought over from Europe by a priest in the 1880s.

It felt like only yesterday that she was told these things, sitting here in this very sanctuary, taught by the most unlikely source, or so she thought at the time. If she closed her eyes, she knew she could picture him, hear his melodic voice, and smell the pine-scented soap he used. She felt his presence here much more than on the street outside of his childhood home, and she couldn't help but rove her gaze about the congregation, searching for those bright blue eyes.

When the Mass ended, she stayed behind and watched as the altar servers, two boys and two girls, tidied the altar and extinguished the candles. She felt at peace here despite, or perhaps because of, the feeling of his presence. More than likely, the feeling came from a lifetime of attending Mass and the knowledge that no matter the language, the readings, the prayers, and the rituals were the same everywhere in the world. She listened to the same gospel and said the same prayers that Nicola and his family had heard and said earlier that day at Our Lady of the Roses. She missed them, but she felt close to them here as she had always felt close to her own parents every Sunday morning all those years ago when she was here, and they were back home.

Ten minutes went by, quietly and peacefully, before Marta stood to leave. She genuflected at the end of the pew and turned toward the doors at the back of the church. An odd feeling spread across her, like the feeling of one's breath on the back of the neck, and her body gave a light shiver. She stopped and searched the church, certain that she would find someone's eyes on her, but she saw no one.

She shook off the feeling and left the church, unaware of the man standing in the shadows who watched her leave.

The rain began shortly after Marta returned home, falling lightly at first and then increasing to the constant, tapping cadence of a snare drum. She busied herself in the house, making a large pot of minestrone for her dinner with enough to eat for a few days. She remembered how convenient it was to have a freezer that held more than a tub or two of gelato and looked forward to freezing several servings of the soup for later.

She laid out her suit and underclothes for the next day and double checked the train schedule. Since she would be traveling between Baltimore and Washington only a few times on this trip, it was less expensive to take the train than to rent a car. Besides, she had never driven a car in either city and hadn't driven a car at all here since the day…

Marta sighed heavily as memories began to weigh her down. She felt his presence everywhere even here where they had spent no time together. Was it a mistake to come back? Was she tempting fate? She closed her eyes and leaned back into the chair that sat in front of the little writing desk where Zia Isabella wrote her weekly letters to her family back home. Marta had claimed the desk as her workstation on this trip and felt her aunt's strong hand squeezing her shoulder as her voice delivered a warning.

You are playing with fire, Marta. He is not worth ruining your life and throwing aside your dreams. Open your eyes and see the truth that is before you.

Now, as then, she felt a tear slide from the corner of her eye.

"Why am I here, Zia Isabella? Why did I return? Please, tell me what I am to do now that I am here?"

Marta, no longer the same twenty-two-year-old to whom the warning had been spoken, wished her aunt could advise her now and answer her questions, but no answers came. She ate dinner to the sounds of the television then went to bed early only to be pulled back into the past by the memories she was unable to restrain as her dreams took over her mind.

10 June 1983

It was hot today, very hot. Zia Isabella sent me to the market, and I walked home with the groceries bouncing in the bags I carried while sweat dripped down my back. From the open windows I could hear Huey Lewis telling about the heart of rock and roll and Cindy Lauper singing about girls wanting to have fun. My university flat mates and I often listened to American music, but this summer, I am certainly getting a lesson in all areas of pop culture. MTV and Saturday Night Live are teaching me things I did not learn at university, including how to dress with more color and style. The double tank tops I wore and the black rubber bracelets that covered my right arm would have been laughed at back home, but I felt good, sexy even, something my mother would have frowned at.

I was nearing our street when I heard footsteps hurrying behind me. I smiled as I turned, sure I would see Paul running to help me with my load. Even though Paul is younger than me by five years, he and I have fallen into a comfortable friendship over the past week, and I like being with him. His parents are sweet and often invite me in for an espresso and a piece of cake or pie, which are so unlike our desserts back home. Dominic is rarely at home and only occasionally intrudes upon my thoughts, usually in those quiet moments before sleep when my mind recalls the way his thumb lightly touched my lip.

Allora, I heard footsteps behind me, and so I turned to look, and my breath caught in my throat at the sight of the two men quickly gaining ground on me. Zio Roberto always warns me to be careful, never to let my guard down, and always to be aware of my surroundings. He even encourages me to do things with Paul, knowing I will otherwise be wandering around alone. I have always taken his advice with a polite smile and promised him I'd be careful, but I see now that I was being foolish. I never considered I would find myself in danger.

His warnings and today's events now replay in my mind like the U2 record I bought at the record shop, spinning the same songs again and again and again. When I turned around, I knew it was too late to heed his warnings. I just stood there and stared at the men. The groceries felt like lead weights in my arms.

One of the men shouted at me, "Hand over your purse. Now!" He had a gun pointed at my chest, and even now, my heart races as I remember it. I looked around for help, but there was nobody there. I wondered where they had gone. Only seconds before, the sidewalks had been filled with people. Even the music coming from the houses had gone silent. The man waved the gun at me and continued to shout orders while at the same time nervously glancing right and left.

The second man made his own demand. He said, "Drop the groceries and give us your purse, lady."

I felt my body begin to quiver. My breathing became shallow, and my heart raced, but I was frozen, unable to follow any of their commands.

"What's wrong with you? Can't you understand English?" said the man with the gun. "Drop them!" I was so scared, but I couldn't do what he said. It was like a dream where I could not move.

Then I heard a shout that said, "Officer, hurry, over here!" I watched the men turn in the direction of the voice. Dominic D'Angelo waved his arms and pointed to us yelling, "Over there. Hurry!"

Dominic then rushed toward us, and miraculously the men ran. If I had not been holding the groceries, I would have crossed myself and said a prayer right then.

I looked at Dominic and asked, "Where are the police?" My voice was shaky, and I felt my chest heaving.

"I made them up," he answered as he looked me up and down.

My heart raced faster, and I told him he could have been shot.

He looked at me and said, "Better me than you."

I felt my legs buckle and the groceries, upon which I'd had an iron grip just moments before, slipped from my hands. I had a vague awareness of apples rolling into the street and the sound of glass breaking at my feet, but my mind was swirling. Strong arms went around me and held me up. I looked into his eyes before passing out.

When I opened my eyes, a crowd of people had gathered. Cradled in his strong arms, I looked from one face to another, searching for understanding. When my eyes met his, I sat up and looked around.

His voice was soothing when he assured me by saying, "They're gone. It's okay."

I worried about the groceries, but a voice said, "I've got them," and I turned to see a little boy holding one bag with the other bag at his feet. The boy said, "Your bottle of wine broke and an egg or two, but everything else is good. Signora Santoro gave me a new paper bag since one of yours was ruined by the wine."

Dominic asked me, "Are you able to get up? Can you walk?" I looked into his Mediterranean eyes and saw that they were filled with concern.

I nodded and pushed myself up onto shaking legs. I told him I was fine and thanked him. I reached for the groceries, but the boy looked over at Dominic as if asking for permission.

Dominic shook his head and said, "I'll get those as soon as I know you can stand."

I felt the blood rise to my cheeks. I wanted the crowd to go away, and that included Dominic. I was embarrassed, and I just wanted to run home and hide like a little girl.

As if he could read my thoughts, Dominic began shooing the onlookers away saying, "She's fine. Thank you all. You can go. Thank you."

It took some coaxing, but he managed to get the crowd to disperse, all except for the boy holding the groceries.

"Thanks, kid." Dominic told him, and I saw him pull a dollar bill from his pocket and hold it out to the boy who shook his head.

The boy told him, "No, thank you, sir. My papà would want me to help just because it's the right thing to do." But as he said it, he never took his eyes from the dollar, and I knew he wanted to take it. So did Dominic.

He said quietly and gently, in a way I didn't know he could, "I know, kid, and you did help. Just take this. Buy yourself a Coke and a pastry."

The boy eyed the dollar for another moment before easing the bag onto the ground and taking the bill, thanking Dominic over and over as he ran toward Vaccaro's.

Dominic asked if I could walk if he carried the groceries.

I said yes a little more testily than I intended. After we'd gone a few paces, I said, trying to sound as gracious as possible, "Thank you."

Then Dominic said more than I've ever heard him say. "You're welcome. Those guys, you're not the first person they've gone after this month. The police'll get them soon. They aren't smart or savvy enough to keep getting away. The problem is, nobody wants to get involved, so everyone just turns their back, and they hit and run before someone even has a chance to call the police."

I thought about the suddenly empty sidewalks and the silenced records and Dominic's rush to help. I said, "You didn't turn your back."

He shrugged and said that he wasn't going to let them hurt me. He glanced quickly at me but didn't meet my eyes.

I tried to formally introduce myself, but he cut me off and said, "You're Marta. Paul's friend."

I smiled and told him, "Paul's a nice boy. I enjoy his company. He's been very kind to me."

Dominic glanced my way again and said, "He likes you, you know, but he's not dumb. He knows you're not gonna fall for him."

I told Dominic that I like spending time with Paul and that he makes me laugh which is the truth.

Dominic didn't say anything to that. He just looked ahead and kept walking, carrying the groceries like he did this sort of thing every day. We walked in silence until we reached the patch of grass in front of Zia Isabella's house. It was not an uncomfortable silence, and I thought, I like the way that my stride matches his. Piero always walks so much faster than I do.

The thought jarred me, and I quickly reached for the groceries.

I thanked him again but felt that it was inadequate. What did one say to someone who possibly saved her life?

I was precluded from having to say more by the swinging open of the front door and Zia Isabella running from the house.

She cried out, "Marta! Eva Santoro just called. Are you all right?"

I assured her that I was fine and that despite losing the wine and some eggs, everything was okay. I began to say something about Dominic's help, but the look in her eyes stopped me, and I felt guilty for causing her such worry. She looked at Dominic, who had not yet handed me the bags, and motioned for him to follow. She wrapped her arms around me and led us into the house.

Dominic seemed too large for Zia Isabella's kitchen though he was not much taller than Zio Roberto. There was something about him that filled the room and made me feel safe, though others no doubt found his muscular build, his quiet demeanor, and his solemn gaze to be discomforting. Zia Isabella thanked him for his help and politely sent him on his way.

"Let me look at you," she said, taking my arms and opening them wide so that she could get a good look. "Grazie a Dio," she said, raising her eyes toward Heaven. "Mi cara, you must be careful, aware. This is not like our little village."

English words would not come, and I found myself crying to her in Italian, "Si, Zia Isabella, lo so. Sono così dispiaciuto." I felt the tears coming before I could stop them. I wanted so desperately to let her know just how sorry I was and how afraid I felt. I rambled in Italian, telling her how I heard them coming, how I saw them when I turned, about the gun, how Dominic had yelled and frightened them away, and how I had fainted but awoke quickly to find a crowd of people gathered around. She listened, her lips pursed and her eyes full of sympathy. At the mention of Dominic's name, a shadow crossed her face, but she hid it almost instantly, and I continued, unable to control my words as they tumbled out of my mouth. When I finished, I fell into her arms and wept.

I heard her words in Italian. "Thank the Lord that man finally did something good."

Chapter Three

The train ride back from Washington gave Marta a good chance to look over the notes from her meetings and send some emails to the curator at the Uffizi. Marta was pleased with what The National Gallery was willing to offer, and she thought her supervisor would be as well. There was still a sticking point or two that they had to work around, but it had been a productive day. They would take a day or two to fine tune both of their offers before meeting again.

Marta had taken the time after her meeting to browse around the museum. It was her first visit since Zio Roberto and Zia Isabella took her there all those years ago. She marveled at Rubens' masterpiece, *Daniel in the Lion's Den* and Castagno's *David with the Head of Goliath*. She studied Leonardo da Vinci's *Ginevra de'Benci*, recalling her trip to Paris where she saw *The Mona Lisa*. As different as the two portraits were, Marta loved studying the similarities—the shape of their faces, their noses and chins, their serious expressions, the colors in the backgrounds, and the infringement of the backgrounds on the women.

Marta stared, perplexed by some of the sculptures, and nearly wept at the beauty of Thomas Cole's *Voyage of Life* series, wondering just where in the series she was these days, grateful for all that she had seen and experienced in life yet longing for the carefree, innocent days of her past and not willing to accept that she was now on the opposite end of the line. She spent quite some time sitting on a bench, mesmerized by Monet's *The Japanese Footbridge*, and she decided that she and Zia Isabella had been wrong so long ago when they said that this museum could not compare to the Uffizi. Though tremendously different in architecture and layout, both museums held impressive displays that could keep the artistically inclined busy for days, pondering the techniques, skill, and meaning behind the works of art within each building.

As she walked across the National Mall toward the metro that would take her back to the train station, Marta looked around at the young city. Compared to Florence or Verona, and certainly Rome, Washington was still in its infancy. The modern buildings intrigued her, especially the capital's own castle, the headquarters of the Smithsonian. Though unlike Italian castles, it did bear the resemblance of many castles she had seen elsewhere in Europe, and she wondered why it was built in such fashion when medieval castles were ancient and crumbling by the time Washington was constructed, and certainly by the time the Smithsonian was established. She'd have to look into that at a later time.

She nearly fell asleep on her ride back to Baltimore, the swaying of the train lulling her into a comfortable repose. When her phone rang, she found herself jolting upright and blinking her eyes, trying to get her bearings. She looked at her phone and sucked in a short gasp, hastily pressing the button to connect.

"Nicola? Is everything all right?" she asked in English, having by now morphed back into her younger self, at ease with the language.

"Ciao, Mamma. Si, everything is fine," her son answered in Italian. "How is America?"

She settled back down into the cushioned seat and spoke in her native tongue. "Molto bon. I was worried when I saw that it was you. It is late there."

"Not very late. You are already on American time if you think ten o'clock is late."

Marta laughed. "Or maybe I'm just getting old."

"Impossible," he answered. "You will never get old."

"How is Alexandra? The children?"

"They are all fine. Alexandra is feeling very well. She has her energy back and is cleaning everything. Yesterday, she polished my work boots before I went back out into the field."

"It is too early for that. She better not have my grandchild while I am away."

"I will be sure to tell her that," he said with a chuckle. "When is your first meeting?"

"It was today," she said, not bothering to remind him that she both told him and emailed him her schedule. He was just like his father with too much on his own mind to remember anything she told him that was not about the vineyard or the wine. "I am on the train now heading back to Baltimore."

"And it went well?"

"Si, it went well. We are not in total agreement yet, but we will get there."

"And what did you do your first weekend back in America?"

Marta thought about the mundane chores she did in the house and the walk she took through the neighborhood. "Not very much. It was a tiring journey. I rested."

"There you go again, thinking you are old."

"I didn't say that," she protested. "I said I was tired."

"You did not see any of your friends you have been in contact with?" She heard the taunt in his voice and wondered why he had such a hard time believing she had friends in America but knew it was because she didn't have any and would have mentioned them if she had.

She hesitated for a moment, not wanting to admit the truth. "Not yet. I was busy getting the house in order."

"Was it not ready when you arrived? I gave orders for it to be ready." His voice hovered between concern and anger.

"No, it was fine, but I wanted to make up my own bed and unpack my things, and I wanted to choose my own groceries."

"I know how little you eat when you are alone. You are eating, aren't you?"

As if in agreement with Nicola and reminding her how she had neglected it, her stomach growled, and she wondered when the child had taken on the role of the parent. "I am eating, cara. Do not worry." She heard another voice. "Is that Alexandra?"

"It is. She just finished putting the children to bed."

"Ciao, Mamma," Alexandra's voice floated across the room. "Nicola, they are waiting for you to kiss them goodnight."

"Please tell her hello for me." Marta heard the announcement for Penn Station. "I have to go Nicola. We are at the station. Please give many hugs and kisses to everyone."

"Si, ti amo, Mamma. Be safe."

After she disconnected the call, Marta hurried to gather her things and exit the train. When she descended the steps onto the platform, she caught a glimpse of a man ahead of her. He wore a dark grey suit and had wavy brown hair. He walked with confidence and purpose, and his gait seemed so familiar, she almost lost her footing on the platform as she tried to keep up with him. The stumble brought her to her senses. She had been seeing things, imagining that he was there when there was no evidence that he even still lived in the city.

Summoning an Uber, Marta made her way back to the house, wondering what, if anything, she should do about locating him.

15 June 1983

My grasp of the language I've been learning for most of life is finally taking hold, and I find myself able to speak, create descriptions, and convey my feelings more easily with each passing day. Paul's ease and natural curiosity has a lot to do with that. He isn't afraid to ask questions and is always willing to teach me new things.

This morning, he had me try a popsicle. It's frozen, flavored ice, and eating it made me miss gelato even more. No matter how fast I licked it, it melted faster. I kept licking the sweet, sticky liquid off the back of my hand, but the popsicle kept melting faster than I could eat it. I asked Paul, "Who thought of freezing colored sugar water and selling it as food?"

Paul was surprised, and it was obvious that he assumed I'd like it. He said, "These are considered a major summertime food group around here." His lips and tongue were stained red, and he seemed to have no trouble with the same dripping mess I was trying to conquer.

I told him that this was not food as my last bite fell from the stick and plopped on the white step where we sat. I kicked it into the little patch of grass just as a shadow fell over us. I looked up into Dominic's scowling face.

I apologized quickly, still lapsing into Italian because he made me so nervous. I offered to get water and clean the step, but when I started to rise, Paul stopped me by placing his hand on my thigh. It was not a forward gesture. He just meant for me to not get up. He said not to worry about the quickly melting red ice, saying it wouldn't hurt anything.

I gazed up at Dominic and found him looking at me with a strange combination of puzzlement and amusement. My stomach twisted in knots when he asked, "Why is it that every time I see you, you have food on your face?"

My face burned, and I felt indignation rise to a dangerous level. I snapped, "How come every time I see you, you are looking and acting like you are il capo and we are contadini?"

Dominic laughed. It was the first time I'd seen him laugh, and it caught me off guard.

Through his laughter, he asked, "What did you just say? Did you just call me a captain, or was it a piece of—" I won't write the word he used.

Paul answered for me, telling his brother that il capo means the boss or leader. Paul said. "Don't you ever pay attention to anything? Nonna used to call Nonno that when she was mad at him for giving her orders." I wanted to laugh at that, but I find it hard to laugh when Dominic is nearby. What is it about him that makes me so nervous?

Dominic asked what I had called myself, and I told him that I did not call myself anything. I rose from the stoop and tried to tell him what I said, but my emotions were blocking any rational thought and caused me to forget all the words I knew.

Paul asked if I meant to say he treated us like slaves, but I shook my head. I told him it was the word for farm workers or poor villagers.

"Peasants," Dominic said with a smile. He leaned back against the metal railing that bordered the step, looking amused. "I hardly think of you as a peasant. And you," he looked at Paul, "are just a nuisance." He turned his gaze back to me and asked why I hang out with his brother anyway.

I told Dominic that it's because Paul gives me something to laugh at, and I meant it in a good way, but Paul turned red and looked at me with such hurt. He accused us of making fun of him, and then said to me, "You think I'm just someone to laugh at?"

I saw the pain in his eyes and knew that I had said something wrong, but the words were right, or I thought they were. I tried to tell him no and reached to touch his arm, but he yanked it away and stormed up the steps.

After the door closed, Dominic shook his head. He told me, "He's still such a kid. I just don't get what you see in him."

I inhaled deeply through my nostrils and clenched my jaw. I insisted, "He is not a kid. He is almost a man, and no doubt more of a man than you are." I turned to go, but Dominic grabbed my arm. I felt his fingers squeeze my bare flesh, and a new feeling made its way up my arm. I couldn't name it, but it made me feel...curious, I suppose, and not at all frightened.

His voice was calm and almost remorseful when he apologized and said he hadn't wanted to make me angry. I turned back toward him.

I told him quietly but sternly to unhand me, and he immediately let go of my arm.

He continued to say he was sorry and then blew out a stream of air and shook his head. Before I could turn to leave, he asked me to get a Coke with him. I could hardly believe what I'd just heard.

I squinted and scrutinized his expression. I wondered what we could possibly have to talk about. My head was commanding me to walk away, but from somewhere else deep inside, a voice was imploring me to say yes. I questioned him about what he meant, and he suggested we walk down to Café Gia and get something to drink.

I knew I should say no. From what I gather, Dominic isn't very popular in the neighborhood. Why, I do not know, but it seems he's been in some trouble. I tried to get Paul to tell me, but as much as he complains about his brother, he is quite protective of his brother and will not speak of whatever it was Dominic did. Asking Zia Isabella is out of the question. Her body language the day Dominic brought me home told me that he is, as Americans say, off limits.

Still, I found myself looking into those eyes, and saying okay.

Dominic walked beside me when we walked down the street. Where the sidewalk narrowed, he stopped and allowed me to pass. He had perfect manners, and that intrigued me even more.

At an outside table, a server delivered a Coke for him and a glass of wine for me.

Dominic made a gesture at my glass and said it was too hot to drink wine.

"It is never too anything for wine," I assured him. I told him what Papà always said, "due dita di vino e una pedata al medico."

He asked me what that meant, and I said, "In English, it says, two drops of wine, and we can kick the doctor out the door." I smiled recalling how Papà loves to announce this when he opens a new bottle of wine fresh from the cellar. I suppose those grapes and that wine are a part of me even if I do wish to leave them behind.

Dominic laughed, and I noticed for the first time that he has dimples in his cheeks. He said, "Wine instead of apples, huh?" Then he asked if I grew up on a vineyard, "or something."

When I didn't smile or laugh, his expression changed to one of disbelief. He said, "Hold on. You grew up on a vineyard?"

What is this, "hold on" that Americans say? Hold onto what?

I told him that I live on a vineyard named Belle Uve, and he looked like it was hard to believe.

What he said next was so strange. He said, "I guess I never thought about there being actual vineyards in Italy these days." He explained that he assumed everything was modernized and streamlined, and he asked, "Does your family actually grow the grapes and make the wine?"

Can you imagine such a question?

I told him, sí, the vineyard has been in our family for hundreds of years.

Dominic sat back with a pensive look on his face and asked if there are a lot of vineyards in Italy.

I asked, "Have you never been to Italy?" I was more than surprised. Italy was his homeland. How could he never have gone?

But he shook his head and said that it's expensive to go to Europe and that his family could never afford that. I tried to detect resentment, but there was none.

I asked, "What does your family do? What business do they have, I mean."

Dominic looked at me with one eye partially shut as if my question confused him. He told me that his family does not have a business. His father works at a plant named G M, and his mother works part-time (what is this part-time?) at the American Can Company.

I didn't know or understand what he meant. I asked what he meant about part-time and if his mother works outside of their home.

Again, he gave me a strange look. He said that his mother went to work when he went to high school. She works only three days a week. He said it was the only way they could send him and Paul to Catholic school.

I was further surprised. His parents had to pay to send them to school!

Dominic shook his head at me and said, "You really don't know what the real world is like, do you?"

I didn't like the way he said that. I was embarrassed and felt like a child. I said, "I've been to many places in the world—Florence, Rome, Paris, Vienna. We traveled at the end of the season every year, and I traveled while at university."

And he said, "Must be nice to have money."

I heard no malice in his tone, but I was still irritated by his words and blurted out, "What does money have to do with it? My family owns a vineyard." I tried to maintain the same neutral tone, but I saw his brow rise.

His tone was nonbelieving and this time, insulting when he said, "And you don't have money?"

I felt my emotions bubbling to the surface and, as I always do when I'm upset, I began to ramble. I said, "We have all we need. We have each other and the vineyard and friends and..." Then I stopped, realizing that I was suddenly crying, and I did not know why. I grabbed a napkin from the metal box on the table and dabbed at my eyes.

"I'm sorry," Dominic said. His voice was soft and gentle. He went on, "I guess I presumed... Anyway, I didn't mean to make you cry. I'd never want to hurt you, Marta."

My heart stopped. There was something in the way he said my name that made me look up at him. For a moment, I was lost in those big blue eyes. They were a sea of emotion, and I felt swept away in their waves. I felt him touch me. His hand lightly caressed my bare arm, and for a moment, I could not breathe.

I quietly told him that I thought I should go though I did not want to leave.

Dominic pulled his hand away, and I felt a sudden chill, even though the hot summer sun was beating on my sweat-soaked back. We walked back in silence, and I found myself trying to memorize every word he said.

When we reached the house, I saw the curtain move and knew that Zia Isabella had been waiting for me. She was not happy with me when I came inside.

The computer screen blinked as it shifted from search page to results, and Marta took a long sip of wine before scrolling through the many links. There were dozens and dozens of men named Dominic D'Angelo. Images of young boys and teenagers filled the gaps between old men and even some tombstones. She could have spent all night combing through the obituaries and the social media links. When she narrowed the search to include *Little Italy*, nobody named Dominic was on the list though there were several D'Angelos. She backed up a page and stared at the original search results. She decided that the LinkedIn profiles might be a good starting point and clicked the link, but before she began scrolling through the names, she sat back and pondered a different approach.

Why had she not thought of this before? She told Nicola that she was connecting with old friends, and she could attempt to do just that. Why jump right into the frying pan? She could ease herself in just as she did the first time, through his brother. After all, she knew Paul had a Facebook page, even if he rarely used it, so maybe there was more information out there in other places.

She tapped on the keys and brought up a new set of results. All the hits she saw on the first page of results were for a comedian. She looked closely at his face but saw no resemblance to the spunky young man she knew, though it would not have surprised her if Paul had grown up to be famous. He had such a confident air and approachable demeanor. People would naturally flock to him. It only took seconds, though, to learn that this Paul D'Angelo was born and raised in Boston. She hit the arrow to continue to the next page, and she was brought up short by one of the results—a YouTube video featuring an interview with Baltimore restauranter, Paul D'Angelo, a lifelong resident of Little Italy.

She watched the video twice, remembering his smile, his laughing eyes, and his kind voice. Nothing had changed. It appeared that he was just as welcoming, charming, and funny as she remembered. That must be an inherit trait for somebody with his name, she mused.

Paul, it seemed, had indeed gone on to college as he planned, studying business, but had dropped out of a local university to study at a culinary school in New York. He returned to Baltimore after spending a year in Sicily and opened his restaurant which was now celebrating its thirtieth year in business.

Two thoughts struck Marta as she watched the video—how did Paul look exactly the same as he did in 1983, and why had he not sought her out when he was in Italy? She sat back in the chair and reached for her wine to take a long, slow drink. That would have been what—1988, '89? It would've been difficult to find someone those days without the financial means to do so. There was no internet, no social media, and no readily available directories that would aid someone in that kind of search. With all that in mind, she supposed she could forgive him for not looking for her, and besides, Sicily and Verona were very far apart, and though she was married and living in Florence by then, it was still hours away by boat and then train. Paul would not have known where she was, nor would he have known her last name, but Zia Isabella did… Still, it would have been a time-consuming and expensive search, and it appeared that Paul had made good use of his time in Italy.

She picked up her phone and sent a text to Antonella to let her know that she had tracked down Paul. She was opening the Pandora's box at her friend's insistence, but she was worried that she was making a mistake. Perhaps she should not have shared her secret with Antonella.

Perhaps she should have just left that box closed with all of the enigmas it contained. It occurred to her that it was not too late. She did not have to see Paul. But she knew she would. Just by coming here, she had set the wheels in motion.

She looked at the clock on the wall and was shocked to see how late it was. The realization made her yawn, and she closed the laptop and headed upstairs to bed.

Tomorrow is going to be an interesting day, she thought as she drifted off to sleep.

Chapter Four

People went in and out of the constantly swinging door. Marta's seat by the window gave her the perfect view through which to study the building and its patrons. The building was not old, and she thought she remembered a different business in that same place all those years ago. Overflowing flower boxes adorned the lower windows as well as the replica iron balconies outside the upper windows, and the front facade had been replaced with a yellow, arched doorway reminiscent of Sicily. Marta could feel the Old-World charm as she gazed across the street and watched the patrons entering and exiting through the arched doorway.

Many were businessmen in suits and ties, and there was a fair number of women in business attire as well. There were a couple groups of young women, and the occasional mother or nanny with youngsters in tow. Some dined in, and others left only a few minutes after they arrived, carrying take out containers and bags with the name of the restaurant on them—Terra E Mare, in English, Land and Sea.

"Would you like to see the dessert menu?"

Marta turned to the waitress and smiled. "No, but thank you. Just the check, please."

In Italy, dessert would have been expected, along with another glass of wine or an after-dinner drink, perhaps limoncello to aid in digestion, and then a platter of fruit to finish the meal. Marta would have been expected to linger and granted plenty of time to finish her wine and allow her food to settle. In America, eating was not always treated as a casual pastime to be savored and enjoyed, and Marta always wondered if Americans even tasted the food they hurriedly spooned into their mouths, one large helping after another with barely enough time to chew and swallow. She learned quickly that summer of long ago, that there was no need to ask for the check in restaurants outside of Little Italy. It would be brought the moment the waiter or waitress decided one was finished eating, sometimes even when the desserts were still being consumed. It was an appalling practice that she still had trouble overlooking.

The decision to not order dessert today had nothing to do with a rush to end the meal and get back to something else, nor did she have a pressing engagement. She simply did not want to be too full when dinnertime arrived. She wanted to taste as many of Paul's menu items as she could, and while she could have made her large meal of the day the noon meal, as she would have done at home, she wanted to do a bit of a study before she went to Paul's restaurant. She wanted to see how popular the restaurant was with her own eyes instead of just relying on the glowing reviews on Trip Advisor. She also needed to become familiar with the place from the outside so that she didn't feel so nervous once she was on the inside. She smiled when the waitress returned, paid the check, and glanced once more out the window at the restaurant across the street.

Back at the house, the hot, humid afternoon dragged, and Marta resorted to turning on the air conditioning, hearing her Zia Isabella's admonishment in her head. From the cool refuge of the house, Marta spoke to the National Gallery on the phone, sent some emails, and went through boxes in the attic. She was surprised to find a box of things that belonged to her— some clothes, a pair of shoes, a teddy bear with a purple bow, and a stack of photos she wasn't ready to look at. She held the bear out and smiled sadly. She hugged the bear tightly as she recalled the haunting conversation with her aunt.

When Marta had returned from Café Gia with Dominic, Zia Isabella was sweeping ferociously, and Marta knew something was wrong. When she asked her aunt if she was upset about something, the woman had tossed the broom aside and told Marta that she had no idea what she was doing, spending time with "uomo di cattiva reputazione." Marta wondered why Dominic was a man of ill repute, but she decided not to pursue that.

Instead, Marta assured her aunt that there was nothing going on between Dominic and herself, but Zia

Isabella refused to calm down. When she said that Dominic was persona cattiva, Marta knew that whatever he had done, it had been unforgiveable as far as her aunt was concerned. Marta couldn't stand it anymore. She needed to know.

"Per favore, Zia Isabella, please tell me what he did. Why does seeing him upset you so?"

Even after forty years away from Italy, Zia Isabella was able to spew more Italian idioms and insults than Marta knew possible. Most of them were common names and ways to refer to a person one did not like, but two phrases uttered consecutively made Marta stop in her tracks. "Ha rubato una macchina" and "ferito un bambino." Dominic had stolen a car and had hurt a child.

Marta remembered the very one-sided conversation well. She had not known how to react to Zia Isabella and had not known what or how to feel about Dominic. She'd never known anyone who had stolen a car, or anything else for that matter, and certainly not someone who had hurt a child. There had to be more to the story, especially since Dominic was not in prison. For the time being, it seemed best to just reassure her aunt that there was nothing between them. At the time, there wasn't.

20 June 1983

Early this morning, I set out for the bus station to catch the navy line to Lombard Street where I

could then catch the purple line to the Baltimore
Museum of Art. There was an exhibit that I had not
had time to see on my first visit, and I wanted to see
it before it moved on. I stretched my neck to look
down the street, but I didn't see the bus yet, and I was
growing impatient.

It was then that I heard a familiar voice asking,
"Where are you headed?"

With what I know now, or the bits and pieces of it
anyway, I should have been afraid, but I wasn't. I
turned toward the man standing beside me and
offered him a tentative smile.

I explained that I was going to the Baltimore
Museum of Art to see an exhibit I was interested in.

Dominic said, "I'm heading that way myself."
He didn't offer any more information, and I didn't
ask. I thought it more prudent to not get involved in
his business.

I told him that the bus was late, and he said, "It
usually is."

I was grateful when the bus pulled up to the stop,
and we climbed aboard, but I felt ill at ease when I
realized the bus was almost full. I took a seat, the last
open one, and he stood next to it and gripped his
hand on the upper rod to keep himself steady. At the
next stop, the woman next to me excused herself, and
I let her by. I hesitated before moving over into the

empty seat, and he looked at me with a raised brow. I nodded but looked out the window when he sat down.

He would not let me be and asked, "You like art, I take it?"

I turned to look at him and nodded. I answered with the explanation, "Si, I will be working in Il Uffizi when I get back home." After Piero and I get married, I should have added, but did not.

He said, "I've always admired artists. I have no talent myself." And then he asked if I have any talent in art.

I told him I have some and gestured toward the camera in my lap. I said that I prefer photography and told him, "My talent lies more in my eye than in my hand."

"I've never heard it put that way before," he said.

A very pregnant woman climbed aboard, and Dominic immediately stood and offered her his seat which she took graciously, thanking him profusely. I wondered how someone with such impeccable manners could have committed the type of egregious crimes Zia Isabella had alluded to.

At the next stop, we both exited and began walking in the same direction. I could see the purple bus ahead and thought about running to catch it, but it was already too hot to exert the energy.

Dominic asked if that was my bus, and before I could answer, he began to run, waving his arms and shouting for the bus to wait.

I hurried and arrived in time to see Dominic hand the man a folded bill. Dominic gestured for me to get in, nodded, then told me to have a nice time at the museum before stepping out of the way so that the driver could close the doors. I made my way to an empty seat, dumbfounded by his actions.

Sometime later, I found myself gazing at a series of photographs, admiring the creativity of the composition, when I suddenly felt his presence beside me. For the first time, I was afraid. Had he followed me? Was I to be his next victim? Should I run? Scream? Find help? All of these thoughts ran through my mind.

He spoke, saying, "After my meeting, I had nowhere to go, so I thought I'd find you and have you show me this exhibit you came all the way here to see."

I was at a loss for words, so I just pointed to the photographs on the wall by Mark Klett.

Dominic tilted his head and stared at the photographed nature scenes. He asked me if I like to take photos of nature.

I answered, "Sometimes." I like to take photographs of everything, but nature is my favorite. Perhaps because I grew up on a rural vineyard and find such peace there even though I do love city life. I am beginning to realize more and more how much the vineyard means to me.

We walked to the next set of photos and admired them together.

Dominic surprised me by asking, "Can I see them sometime? Your photos?"

I told him no, taken by surprise. I explained that I don't have any with me. They're all back in Italy.

He nodded and said, "Maybe you could take some. There are places to find nature shots even in the city. I could show you some places."

I answered, "Thank you, but I prefer to work alone." That is the truth, but it is also an excuse to avoid spending more time with him. Still, I could feel the weight of the thought that it might be nice to have a picture of him...

When we reached the end of the exhibit, we stood looking at each other uncomfortably until Dominic finally looked down at his watch and asked if I had eaten. He said he was starving.

I suddenly realized I, too, was quite hungry and said so before I could stop myself.

"I've got a great place in mind. I think you're going to love it. Come on."

Despite my misgivings, I followed.

We walked for a little more than ten minutes before taking another bus. This time, it was much less crowded, and we sat together. Dominic asked a lot of questions about my studies and my photography. I had so many questions of my own, but I refrained from asking. It was a second bus ride and another ten-minute walk before we stood outside the gate of the Maryland Zoo. I looked at Dominic.

I said, "I thought we were going to lunch."

He pointed to a curbside truck nearby, and I hurried to keep up with him as he headed in its direction. He asked me, "Ever had a corn dog?"

I shook my head.

"You're in for a treat then," he said, ordering two corn dogs and paying for both. I didn't protest. I was too busy staring at the breaded tubular food items lying on some kind of rotating cooker with a stick protruding from one end of each concoction. I took the one that Dominic handed to me, but he warned that it might be hot, so I blew on it for a moment before he said, "Come on. We'll eat inside."

Again, he paid for me, and we entered the zoo.

The corn dog was really good and actually reminded me of some of our foods back home. We ate and walked through the zoo, pointing and laughing at the animals. I took my camera out of my bag and took photos of elephants and bears and monkeys. I even took a photograph of Dominic pretending to be a chimpanzee, and he playfully threatened to have it destroyed if I got it developed. I was careful not to focus on his face just in case it happened to get developed and Zia Isabella found it.

"Which one is your favorite?" he asked me.

I had to think about it before answering, "Maybe the bears."

"Mine, too," he said, and his gaze held mine while a monkey swung from tree to tree on the other side of the cage. Dominic slowly reached his hand to just beneath my lips and gently caressed my chin. "You don't have any food on you this time," he said quietly, and I felt a thousand hairs stand on my arms and legs. My stomach twisted, and a warm feeling rose into my chest.

I told him that it was getting late and that Zia Isabella would be worried if I didn't get back soon.

Dominic nodded and reached for my hand. I let him take it and held onto him as we made our way back to the entrance.

Before we left, I asked to use the toilet, and he told me that he had to do the same. When I went back to find him, expecting him to be waiting for me already, he was nowhere in sight. I was just beginning to worry when I spotted him coming from a building across the way. He was holding a bag.

He said, "Let's go" without mentioning his purchase, and a sudden thought crossed my mind. I could not help but wonder if he had purchased whatever was in the bag. I worried that perhaps he had not paid for it but had stolen it. He seemed to have money, but... Allora, the item was in a bag, so he must have paid for it, I reasoned, but I was unsure.

Those thoughts led to another whole series of thoughts, each one more ominous than the last. By the time we got to the bus stop, my heart was beating wildly, and I was sweating from every pore.

Dominic asked if I was okay and said, "You seem nervous or something."

I told him I was fine. I looked down at the bag and finally asked, "What's in there?"

He smiled and just said, "You'll see."

The buses were crowded again, and Dominic helped an elderly lady to the only empty seat. I stood, hand on the rod, and watched him. Perhaps Zia Isabella is wrong. This man could not have committed a crime and could never hurt anyone. It makes no sense. I wrestled with my thoughts, and still wrestle with them now, and I wrestled with my conscience until we reached the final bus stop.

Before we began walking, Dominic reached into the bag and pulled out a stuffed bear with a purple bow.

He said, "A memento to remember the day" and handed me the bear. Then he said, "Thank you for trusting me."

His words, his tone, and the look he gave me told me that my trust meant more to him than anything I could ever give him.

It was seven o'clock when Marta took her seat at the small table for two. Candles glowed on starched white tablecloths and from the sconces adorning the yellow columns that sectioned off rooms throughout the restaurant. There were no murals or framed scenes of Il Colosseum or Il Capital like so many Italian restaurants outside of Italy had. The simple décor, the cracked yellow walls, and the scents that hung in the air—garlic and oregano but also grilling steak and sautéing seafood—made the restaurant feel authentic without the characteristic pictures and paintings. The wait staff looked proud to work there, and Marta could understand why. Her heart flooded with happiness for Paul.

"Wine, Signora?" A sommelier stood by the table with a bottle of white and a bottle of red wine in each hand. "We offer a complimentary glass while you look over your menu."

"How nice. Red, please." Marta wondered if the complimentary wine would taste like vinegar, but she had a feeling that Paul would do better than that. The sommelier poured her wine and waited for her to taste it, and she was not disappointed.

"Oh my," she said. "This is, this is eccezionale." She was reminded of the story of the wedding feast at Cana, where the head wine steward remarked that the good wine is always served first. "Where is this from?"

"A vineyard near Verona, signora."

Her heart skipped a beat. "May I see?" she asked pointing toward the bottle. He held it out for her to see the label, and she felt a flutter of disappointment. "Allora, La Dama."

"You know it, signora?"

"Si, it is very near my home. It is good, very good, but not ours."

A look of surprise crossed his face. "Yours? A vineyard?"

"Si, my son's. His Amarone is an award-winner."

"And the name of the vineyard?"

"Belle Uve."

"Beautiful Grape," he said. "I am embarrassed to say that I am not familiar with it. Does he have an American distributor?"

"He does, but I will have to ask him the name."

"No need. I will look for it. You have my word." He bowed and walked away.

Marta's meal was as exceptional as the wine. The swordfish rolls were perfectly breaded and grilled, and the fresh, toasted bruschetta melted in her mouth. The Pasta Alla Norma, with its blend of tomatoes, aubergines, garlic, basil, and salted ricotta was a veritable dream come true for pasta lovers. Just as she would have at a restaurant back home, Marta also ordered a secondi,

Falsomagro, beef served in a roll with prosciutto, cheese, and sausage rolled around hard-boiled eggs. She skipped the insalata and went right to something sweet. When she asked for the dessert menu, she inquired about the owner from the waitress.

"Is Signor D'Angelo here tonight?"

"Yes, may I deliver a message?"

She'd thought about it all day. What would she say if asked this very question?

"Si, please tell him that Marta is here, and that Zia Isabella would be proud."

A few minutes later, instead of being given the dessert menu, a man in a white shirt appeared at her table holding out a plate.

"I know it's not your birthday, but it is a day to celebrate."

She looked from the torta Setteveli to the man holding it and began to cry.

If Marta had not been raised on a vineyard, she might have felt the effects of the second bottle of wine that they shared. Instead, she felt elated, like she had just awoken to find that her dream was a reality. They talked and laughed and shared news of their lives—her marriage to Piero and all that Nicola had accomplished with the vineyard, and Paul's marriage to Sophia, a girl he met his first year of college before he left for culinary school. They had five children and three grandchildren, including twins. Most of his children worked in the restaurant, including his youngest daughter, a twin, Antonia, who had been her waitress.

"I can't believe it's been thirty-six years," Paul said, shaking his head. "You look just the same today as you did the day you stopped in front of my house and I asked your name, Marta Marta."

She laughed. "I look thirty-six years older. But you, Paul, you look more handsome than I remember."

"Don't tease me. You never had eyes for me."

So, he had opened the door after all. She was not sure he would.

"How is he?" She asked boldly, hoping the news was good.

"He has done well for himself," Paul said. "There was only one time in his life that I saw him truly happy, and that was a short summer a long time ago, but he is happy now with his many boys surrounding him."

Marta's heart was pierced by both the memory and the mention of his many boys, and she was admittedly jealous, but she did not reply to Paul's comment about that summer. "Oh? He has many children? And where is he now? What is he doing?"

"No, the boys are not his children. He and Sally run a shelter for troubled youth. Some of the boys are sent there after committing a crime and stay for a while. Others go in and out, hour by hour or day by day."

Marta tried to keep her attention focused on his words, but there was one word in particular that grabbed her attention and almost caused the wine glass to slip from her hand. "Sally. So he is married then? I remember a girl named Sally who worked at the movie house. Perhaps this is the same one?"

Paul laughed heartily. "No, no, Sally is Salvatore DeLuca. He's an attorney. He represents a lot of the kids."

"Are he and Dominic…?"

Again, Paul laughed from his gut. "Are you kidding me? Sally's married to Rosa's daughter, Millie. Remember her?"

"Older than me, right?"

"Yeah, she and Sally are both older. Sally would've been a law student when you were here. Dominic never married." He sighed and held steady her gaze for several moments before he said, "He only ever loved one woman."

Again, Marta felt a stab in her heart and chose her next words carefully. "So, this shelter, is it nearby?"

Paul eyed her then nodded slowly. "Yeah, but Marta, there's something you should know."

She felt a lump in her throat. It was bad. She knew it by the way he said it, by the look in his eye. She tried to swallow the lump away, but it remained.

"Dom's sick, Marta. We don't know how much time he has."

Chapter Five

Marta awoke to the sound of the trash truck and clanging metal cans against the back of the truck. She squeezed her eyes tightly together, trying to conjure the melodies of songbirds and children's laughter and Alex's windchimes hanging on the front porch. She pictured her grandchildren, running through the fields, and a bounty of plump grapes glistening with the morning dew. She wanted to be there, to be home, not even at her apartment in Florence, but home—the vineyard—where generations of her family toiled and ate and drank and danced.

Dom's sick, Marta. We don't know how much time he has.

The words broke through, interlopers in her happy thoughts, and she saw Dominic as she once knew him—tall and strapping with wavy black hair, dimples in his cheeks, and blue eyes the color of the sea. She felt his strong hand holding hers, saw the way he looked through the lens of her camera, and tasted the sweet taste of Coca Cola on his lips.

One time. That's all there had been. She had let him kiss her one time, and she knew that she could never let it happen again. If she had, there would not have been a wedding, not to Piero. His kiss felt so good, so right, and she knew it was all wrong. It was wrong then, and it was wrong now. She knew now that there never would have been Nicola, the vineyard would have been sold or left to ruin, Alexandra would not have entered their lives, and her precious grandchildren would not exist.

She moaned painfully as the utterly selfish thought came, unbidden, that had she known what she knew now—about Dominic's illness—she might not have left. All of those things and people she loved the most would not exist, but she would have had a lifetime with Dominic. It was so wrong to even imagine it, yet she could not help it. She didn't want to think it, but there it was.

She heard a scream, so loud and filled with grief that she sat up, eyes wide and heart racing, and then realized the scream was her own. She could not forsake Piero or their child and grandchildren. She had loved him dearly from the moment they first met. She could not imagine all those years without him or all the years without Nicola. To even imagine anything else was a sin.

Suddenly, it all felt too heavy—the guilt, the grief, the regrets. She threw off the quilt as if that could remove the weight, but it was no use. She had a choice to make—to go home and pretend she never saw Paul and didn't know the truth or to go to the address Paul wrote down for her and see him for herself one last time.

She texted Antonella. It was afternoon in Florence, so her friend might be working, guiding tourists along the Ponte Vecchio or entertaining them with the story of David inside La Academia.

Thankfully, it only took seconds for Marta to receive a reply.

"Go see him. Why waste another minute? Instead of worrying, say a prayer of Thanksgiving that you got there before it was too late."

Knowing Antonella was right, Marta got out of bed and stood before the closet, searching for what to wear. Did it really matter? What difference would it make if she wore a dress or slacks or short pants? She was going to see Dominic for the first time in thirty-six years. Nothing she wore would make her feel any better, any more or less self-conscious than she already felt.

She settled on a teal blouse with white slacks, an outfit that outlined her modest curves while accentuating her coloring and small frame and made her feel confident but would feel comfortable in the heat as well. It was not the casual style of the twenty-two-year-old Italian girl who had been trying to fit into an American neighborhood, but she was no longer that same girl and hadn't been since the day she left America, suitcase in hand and tears streaming down her face. Nor would Dominic be the person he was back then, and that was what worried her the most. He was not in a good place when they had fallen in love. Where had his life taken him since then, and had he become someone she would still love or despise?

1 July 1983

I know that what I am doing is not right—to go behind Zia Isabella's back this way, but I have tried, and failed, to reason with her. She does not know about the afternoon at the zoo or the walks around the harbor or watching War Games at Bengie's drive-in. She thinks I am always visiting museums and taking pictures and spending time with Paul and his cousin, Angela. She does not know that I am also seeing Dominic.

This morning, she asked if I had fun last night, and for a moment, I thought she knew. I did not know how to answer until she said, "Rosa was worried that you would be hurt, but Paul and Angela said they would make sure you were okay. Was it fun? Did you fall?"

Oh, I am falling. If she only knew how, she would be furious. I laughed and said, "I did fall at first, but it was not hard. Soon I was skating as fast as Angela."

It was true, but it also was true that Dominic held my hand as I took my first tentative step onto the polished boards. The wheels turned, and I almost fell right on my rear, but Dominic's strong arm held me up until I got used to the feeling of rolling along the floor. Angela skated by me and laughed, hand-in-hand with William Kelly, a man her mother does not approve of. He smokes and drinks beer and speaks with an Irish accent, and even though he is Catholic, he is not good enough for Angela's mother.

Paul skated with friends, but when our eyes met, I knew that he was worried. He does not like the game we are playing, but he is my friend and Dominic's brother, and he quietly plays along.

"Come on, I want to show you something," Dominic said after we skated around and around the rink. I had lost count as we rounded the turns. I could only concentrate on the feel of my hand in his as the spinning ball above cast a kaleidoscope of colored lights on the walls and floor. I let him lead me from the slippery boards to the soda-stained carpet.

"You'll have to take off your skates," he said as he unlaced his black boots with the bright orange wheels. My fingers trembled as I undid the white ones I rented from the man behind the counter. Dominic told me to leave the skates there and follow him. I slipped my feet into my white canvas shoes and my hand into his hand and followed him outside.

The roller-skating rink was not downtown. Angela had to borrow her father's car to drive us outside the city, and Dominic and William met us there. Being away from the city, we were also away from the many lights that lit the night. There was a park with picnic tables across the street, and Dominic and I sat on one of the tables. He pointed to the night sky with his free hand, still holding tightly to my hand with his other.

"You can't see stars like this in the city," he said. "Do you know anything about the stars?"

I nodded but did not answer. I felt as though my throat was closing, like the apple I had eaten earlier that day was lodged inside. I could feel Dominic turn toward me. We sat there, me looking up at the sky and Dominic looking at me. I could feel his gaze, and my stomach grew warm with a rush of activity that felt like a flock of sparrows circling my abdomen. It was a thrilling feeling, intense and consuming like a roaring fire, and my heart began to race.

"Marta," Dominic whispered, and his fingers found the underside of my face just beneath my jawline. They gently caressed my skin, and my breathing caught in my throat. With softness like a sprig of heather, I felt him turning my face toward his, and I swallowed, feeling his touch as my throat rippled.

"Dom! We've got to go!"

The mood was broken by Paul's voice, carried on the night's breeze. I jumped and gasped.

"I already turned in Marta's skates, and I've got yours here. We'll be late if we don't go now," Paul yelled to us.

"Coming," Dominic called, and I heard the curse he uttered beneath his breath. He took my hand, and I went with him.

Standing in the shadows by the car, Angela and William kissed goodbye, and I felt a pang of... I don't know what. Was it remorse or guilt or jealousy? I wanted to be doing that with Dominic. We'd come so close, and I was disappointed, but at the same time, I was relieved. In the back of my mind, I saw Piero's face, and I knew it was better that we had to leave. I knew it, but I still wished it did not have to be so.

Marta stood outside the front door and gazed at the building. The sign on the door read, The Seton Center, and she wondered about the name. The building looked like most of the other buildings in the downtown—a red brick, three story building sandwiched between other brick buildings of varying heights. It looked like it may have been a hotel at one time, based on the design and how there appeared to be a lobby on the other side of the darkened windows. The front door was locked, but a panel of buttons hung next to the door. She pressed the buttons according to the instructions Paul had given her, and a voice answered, "May I help you?"

For a moment, she couldn't find the words, but they slowly came to her. "I'm here to see Dominic. Mr. D'Angelo. Is he available?"

The silence seemed to last an inordinate amount of time, but finally the voice said, "Yes, come in."

A buzzer sounded, and she heard the door unlock. With a shaking hand, she opened the door and stepped across the threshold, certain her life would be forever altered.

A young man approached her, coming from around the counter where hotel guests would have checked in. He reached out his hand to her.

"I'm Tony. Dom's in the gym. Does he know you're coming?"

She shook her head. "No, but Paul told me it was all right to come."

Surprised flashed across his face, but he nodded. "Well then, follow me."

"Prego, I mean, thank you. I'm Marta. We're..." she hesitated, feeling suddenly nervous. "We're old friends. I haven't seen him in years."

Tony gave her an odd look. He opened his mouth and then snapped it shut. He blinked and then said, "I'm sure he'll be happy to see you," but his friendly tone had become strange.

Tony led her down the hall. They passed a large, framed picture of a pastoral scene—flowers in a meadow and the sun beaming overhead—with a quote by the Venerable Fulton Sheen, *You will never be happy if your happiness depends on getting solely what you want. Change the focus. Get a new center. Will what God wills, and your joy no man shall take from you.*

"May I ask you a question," Marta asked. "The name, The Seton Center, where does it come from?"

Tony stopped at an elevator and pressed a button. "It's named after a saint, St. Elizabeth Ann Seton. She was the first American saint, the first saint from Maryland, and is the patron saint of second chances. Dom chose the name. He's big on saints, but you might know that already." Again, his tone was odd.

The elevator opened, and Tony punched in the button for the fourth floor. "There used to be a pool up there, but Dom and Sally thought it would be too expensive and a liability, so they had it converted into a gym. The guys play basketball there. There's a fitness center up there, too. Dom and Sally like to keep us active." Tony grinned as the bell dinged and the doors slid open. He gestured for her to go first.

Marta let Tony lead the way down the hall to the gym. As they neared the room, she could hear shouting and cheering amidst the hard bouncing of a ball on the court. They stopped in the doorway, and her eyes roamed across the wooden floorboards to the bleacher seats. No expense had been spared to create the space. The floor was polished, and the bleachers were well constructed. Hanging on the walls around the gym were signed team posters of the Baltimore Ravens and Orioles as well as the Washington Capitals, Redskins, and

Wizards. She didn't follow sports, other than an occasional football match, but recognized the professional team names on the posters from her past visit.

Hanging alongside them were posters with quotes on them: Psalm 27:3, *Though an army encamp against me, my heart does not fear; Though war be waged against me, even then do I trust,* and one of Marta's favorite quotes by St. Catherine of Sienna, *If you are what you should be, you will set the whole world ablaze!*

Tony raised his hand and pointed toward the bleachers, but she didn't need him to. The minute her eyes fell on Dominic, her heart tripped over itself. "There's Dom."

He looked exactly the same, and she wondered if Paul was mistaken. Certainly, he wasn't sick. He looked just fine.

"Thank you. I appreciate your help." She smiled at Tony and wasn't sure if she wanted him to leave so that she could approach Dominic alone or if she wanted him to take her over to him and spare her from walking across the gym alone. What if he didn't recognize her? What if he didn't even remember her? Just because Paul remembered didn't mean…

All thoughts ceased and she held her breath when Dominic's eyes met hers. He slowly stood. His jaw was open, and she saw him blink twice as if he thought he was seeing things. She saw him mouth her name, and her breathing resumed. She bit her bottom lip and sucked in air while attempting to hold back the tears that welled up in her eyes. She nodded and offered a small smile, suddenly feeling much like the young, uncertain girl she had been rather than the confident woman she had become.

He took his time making his way down the bleachers, and she saw that he struggled with the last step. One of the young men who was watching the game leaped up to help him. Dominic thanked him and clapped him on the back.

"I'm heading back downstairs," Tony said. "It was nice meeting you."

He was gone before she could say goodbye, but that was all right. Marta wasn't sure she could speak. The closer Dominic came to her, the more she could see the pale skin, the worry lines above his eyes, and the thinning of his beautiful hair.

He held his hands out to her as he approached. "Marta, it's really you."

She took his hands in hers, so familiar yet so strange, and felt her smile widen. "It's me, Dominic. It's so good to see you."

"I thought, but then I told myself no, that it couldn't be you. I should have gone to you…"

"What are you talking about?" *Is he hallucinating? Is he sicker than he appears?*

"At the church, a few days ago. Was that you?"

She recalled the feeling of being watched and nodded, quite taken aback. She looked down, realizing they were still holding hands.

It should have been awkward, and she had been sure it would be, but standing with their arms outstretched and their hands clasped felt like the most natural thing in the world. It became even more so when he pulled her to him and wrapped his arms around her. She melted into his embrace and felt the warm rush of tears on her face. She sniffed, and he pulled back to look down at her.

"Are these tears of joy at seeing me or tears of pity because you've talked to Paul?" His voice took on that old familiar tone.

"Can't they be both joy and sadness?" she asked honestly.

Dominic released a long, slow exhale before giving her a short nod. He let go of her and turned back to the boys on the bleachers. "I'll be in my office if anyone needs me," he called over the ruckus of the game.

The boy who had helped him down gave him a thumb's up.

"This way," he said, his hand finding its rightful place on her lower back, as he led her to the elevator.

"Was this a hotel?"

"It was. Sally, did you ever meet Sally?"

She shook her head as the doors opened.

"He and I bought a hotel that was being sold at auction. It was right after the bank crisis. We had it converted. I guess Paul told you about it."

The doors opened on the first floor, and they walked in the opposite direction of the lobby.

"He told me some. He said you'd opened a youth center for troubled boys."

"Boys, men, sometimes it's hard to distinguish." He gestured for her to enter the office, a small former hotel room with a large wooden desk with several large matching filing cabinets, a couch, and two armchairs. He closed the door behind him, and they went to the seating area where Dom sat on the couch and Marta took a seat in one of the chairs. There was a coffee table between them that held several books dealing with intervention, mentoring, and troubled youth.

"The boys come in with the knowledge of men, knowledge they shouldn't have at their ages, and the men come in with the mentality of boys. Somehow, we make it work."

"What do you do? I mean, how do you help them?"

Dominic gave a little shrug. "However we can. We get them jobs, provide training, send some to community college with whatever grant money we can get, and help them find a better way than they've been following. We take them to church and to the doctor and wherever else they need to go to get back on track, or in some cases, to just get on track to begin with."

Marta had noticed a crucifix hanging over the door and a framed quotation above the couch that said, *Jesus, help me to simplify my life by learning what you want me to be — and becoming that person.* The quote was attributed to St. Thérèse of Lisieux.

"You take them to church? How does that go over with them?" She smiled, remembering Nicola as a teenaged boy with a greater desire to sleep on Sunday mornings than to attend Mass.

"Rules are rules. If they want to stay, they have to follow them. That means checking in at the desk every time they come or go, letting us know where they are at all times, following curfew, eating what we serve, participating in group activities, going to therapy, and attending Mass. It's that, or they go to a jail for juveniles."

"What if they're Jewish or Buddhist?" Part of her was playing devil's advocate, and part was genuinely curious. It occurred to her that their interchange felt more like an interview than a conversation between old friends, and she was reminded how long it had been since they were together and talked freely about their hopes and dreams. Then the tone of the conversation changed with Dominic's next words.

"Most of them don't know what they are, and almost none of them have ever entered a church in their lives until they come here. They need it just as I needed it. It was the Church that saved me. That...and you." He leveled his gaze on her as he let his words sink in.

"Me?" she asked, her voice barely above a whisper.

"You," he said with a nod. "I wanted to be a better man, a better person, to make your aunt and uncle see me for something other than my reputation. Eventually, I knew it was too late for us, but for a while, I thought that maybe if I could win them over, of all people, I might actually be able to get beyond my past and the mistakes I made and make something of myself. The more I thought about it, the more I knew that God was calling me to do more than improve myself. He wanted me to help others who'd made the same stupid mistakes I'd made. If I hadn't met you that summer, I might never have found my calling."

"I don't know what to say."

"You don't have to say anything."

They sat looking at each other for several moments before Marta broke the silence. "Tell me about the youth center."

Dominic's eyes sprang to life, sparkling with energy as he told tales about the founding of the center and the young men who occupied it. For more than twenty years, Dominic and Sally had been taking in young men between the ages of twelve and twenty-four, men and boys who would have otherwise fallen through the cracks or become victims of their own circumstances. Their backgrounds were diverse, thrusting them into a variety of situations ranging from parental drug abuse and physical abuse to gang violence, and substance use to many other risk factors and personal screw-ups. The only cases they did not take were sexual abuse victims whose needs were far greater than those the men could provide.

The center provided recreational programs such as daily basketball games and movie nights, academic tutoring, job training and placement, mental and physical health assessment, and safe housing. They even brought in local chefs to give cooking lessons.

"I'm guessing Paul runs some of your classes," Marta said, feeling a rush of admiration for the young man she knew and the man she had reconnected with.

"Runs some of the classes? Are you kidding? Paul spearheads the whole cooking program. Are you familiar with Father Leo Patalinghug?"

"I'm afraid not. Is he at St. Leo's Church?"

"No, but he's a saint in the making." Dominic laughed. "He has a cooking show on cable television, and he lives and operates his nonprofit right here in Baltimore. He helps many previously incarcerated men to find jobs in the restaurant industry. Paul arranges weekly sessions with chefs from all over the city, including Father Leo, and they help the men who really show some promise to get jobs at some of the finest restaurants in Baltimore and beyond. I don't know what we'd do without all of Paul's work and contacts."

"Why am I not surprised?" Marta said with a laugh.

"He always was the good one, you know." A shadow crossed Dominic's face, and Marta's heart felt heavy.

"You're a good one, too, you know," she said quietly. "So good, I had a hard time leaving."

His expression was solemn, and his words were gentle yet painful. "But you did leave. You left, and I had to find a way to keep going. You know, I actually thought there was a chance for me, that what we had was so special that there was a chance for us even after you were gone, but I learned in time that this was God's plan for me."

Marta closed her eyes and wished she could take away the pain, could make up for all the lost time, but time was not on their side. She opened her eyes and looked at Dominic. "I wanted to stay, but I had to go. I made a promise, a commitment. I could not go back on that. And we were young, and it was an exciting time. I wasn't sure if my feelings for you were real or if they were part of the thrill of..." She looked away, embarrassed by the things she had said.

"The sneaking around," he supplied, and she nodded. "Did you love him?"

"Very much," she said, imploring him with her eyes to understand. "Piero was so good to me, so kind and loving, and he was a wonderful husband and father."

"Was?"

Marta nodded and blinked back tears, not sure why she was crying. Piero had been gone for five years, and she had made her peace with his sudden death.

"He had a heart attack five years ago. It was very sudden."

"And you have children?"

"One, a son, Nicola. He is married to an American girl, Alexandra, and they have two little ones and a bambino on the way. Alexandra inherited part of the vineyard when Zia Isabella passed."

"Alexandra? Isa's Alex?"

Marta sucked in a sharp breath. "You know her?"

Dominic nodded. "Very well. She reminded me so much of you..." He looked away, but his emotions were written all over his face as they always had been.

"What? Something is troubling you."

He blew out a long puff of air through his pursed lips. "I miss her."

"Alexandra?"

"No." He turned back toward Marta. "My friend, Isa."

"You've hardly touched your meal," Marta told Dominic.

"I don't have much of an appetite these days."

The seafood restaurant he'd chosen for dinner was within walking distance of the center, and the maître d' knew Dominic by name. He ushered them to a secluded table in the back where they ordered dinner and a bottle of wine. Dominic had insisted that the story of his relationship with her aunt was a long and complicated one and suggested that he tell her over dinner. Marta was stunned by his recounting of the friendship that he and her aunt had developed.

"I am still trying to understand how it began—you and Zia Isabella."

"After you left, I made it my daily mission to prove myself to her. I offered to carry her groceries, wash Roberto's car, and shovel snow from their sidewalk. I decided that I had to win her over in order to find you."

Marta was stunned. He'd wanted to find her?

"What happened? I mean, why..." She couldn't bring herself to ask the question.

"Why didn't I find you?" Dominic shook his head. "I did in a way. When Isa finally came around to accepting that I wasn't so bad after all, you were married. That summer, I knew there was probably someone else, but I had no idea you were engaged until the day you left. You never wore a ring. You never talked about planning a wedding. Why weren't you honest with me from the beginning?"

The pain in his voice would forever haunt her. What had she done? She had convinced herself that she hadn't lied or betrayed or cheated, but hadn't she? Hadn't she done that to both men by omission? She had not been up front with either of them about the other.

"I...I..." Marta closed her eyes, her chin and jaw trembled, and she fought the urge to burst into tears. "I'm sorry," she said quietly. "I never knew it would, we would, I would..." She forced herself to look up at him, to meet his eyes with her own. "I did not know that I would fall in love."

"With your husband?" he asked with incredulity.

"With you," she whispered.

Chapter Six

5 July 1983

Last night was magical. Every year, on 24 June, Firenze celebrates the Feast of St. John the Baptist. I went to the celebration several times while at university. The stores close, special events take place throughout the city, and fireworks light the sky over the Arno after dark. It is a very special day, and I was surprised to know that 4 July in America is celebrated the same way but on a much grander scale. I knew about the fireworks and parades, but I did not know that every town, every city, and every person in the entire country celebrates with picnics and games and crowds of people gathering for fireworks throughout all of the United States. Even Zia Isabella and Zio Roberto were excited to celebrate the birthday of what had been their home for over forty years.

I was excited to be part of it all. The three of us took the bus down to the heart of the city where we were among hundreds of people gathered along the Baltimore Harbor. There were food vendors everywhere and live music that had couples, groups of young people, and children dancing on the docks. I felt like I was back in Florence and swept up in the excitement of it all.

Just before dark, Paul appeared next to our blanket and said, "Angela and I have been looking for you all day. Can you join us?"

I looked over at Zia Isabella and hoped she would not know what I suspected—that Paul and Angela were not alone. Zia Isabella looked at Zio Roberto, and he nodded in approval but said, "It will be chaos when the fireworks end. You will see her home?"

"Yes, sir. We'll make sure Marta gets home."

It still annoys me when they speak like I'm not there, but I didn't say anything. All of my thoughts were of spending this special night with Dominic.

Paul took my hand and led me through the crowd. We made our way along the docks, stepping over blankets and steering clear of the edge of the dock where we could have been knocked easily into the water. It seemed that we walked forever before I spotted Dominic, his anxious eyes scanning the crowd then sparkling with delight when he saw us approaching.

Paul let go of my hand and I ran toward Dominic. He held out his arms, and I fell automatically and without hesitation into his embrace. When he released me, he said, "I prayed I would see you tonight."

He took my hand and pulled me down to the blanket where Angela and William were lying together, her head on his chest, as if they were the only two people there. I said hello, and they managed to smile and act as if they were happy to see me, but I knew that they only saw each other. I wondered what that felt like—to completely lose oneself to another, and I instantly felt guilty for I knew that no matter how much I love Piero, I have never felt that sense of oneness, as if we were the only people in the world. Perhaps in time...

"Are you having fun?" Dominic asked as he cradled my back against his chest. His warm breath tickled the back of my neck, and I felt a shudder go through me. He bent forward to look at my face. "Are you cold? It's at least ninety degrees out here."

I smiled and felt myself blush. "No, I'm very content," I said truthfully and nestled myself into him as his arms squeezed me tightly.

I took some photographs, careful not to betray the truth of my companions, and we settled into a comfortable state of being. We didn't talk. We just watched the people and the boats that floated nearby as the blanket of darkness descended upon us. Without warning, there was a pop and then the sky lit with sparkling lights that cascaded down onto the water. I was mesmerized by the lights of the fireworks, the sounds of their popping, the people cooing, and the smell of Dominic—musky but clean with a hint of aftershave and pine soap—and the feel of his breath on my cheek, our faces pressed close together as we watched the sky.

We stayed that way for the entire show, a long and satisfying display of red, white, and blue accompanied by green, yellow, and pink. It was the most fantastic fireworks show I have ever seen, or perhaps it was just the feeling of seeing it with Dominic. He makes me feel... I can't put it into words, for if I write it down, then I have to face it, and I cannot do that.

Allora! What am I doing? How have I let this happen? Even as I recount this day, I do not know how I have allowed these feelings to grow.

We all walked to the bus in silence, holding hands while shielded among the crowds of people. When we neared the station, Dominic let go, and I felt cold and abandoned. I looked at him and saw the truth in his eyes. We can never be. This, the thing that shall remain without a name, can never happen. My family would not approve, and he knew it. What I still do not know is why.

Dominic insisted upon making sure Marta got back to the house safely. He drove her home in his car, then walked her to the door and saw her inside but made no attempt to stay, retreating back to his car after telling her goodnight. They agreed to meet again the next day when Dominic would tell her about his illness. Tonight, he had said, was for getting reacquainted and acknowledging in the open what they had lost so many years ago, but about which, they had no regrets.

Marta sat in the dark living room, alone except for her memories. They had loved each other. They both knew and admitted it, but too many years had gone by to hold grudges or to speak of what might have been. She had her family, and he had his work, and they both had been happy. Dominic never married though he thought about it often. He had overcome his reputation and was a highly regarded member of the community though he left Little Italy and never returned except to see Paul and their parents—both deceased now—and to eat at Terre E Mare.

When she asked him why he hadn't married, he had simply shrugged and said, "I let the right one get away."

She'd had to look away, knowing him too well, too able to read his expression, his tone, and his mind. But she would not allow herself to feel guilty about it. Dominic made his own decisions, and the life he had created was successful, honorable, and noteworthy. He might not have a wife and offspring, but he had a family with many children who looked up to him. She could see that even in the brief time she was at the center.

The old cuckoo clock whistled when midnight came, but Marta still sat, recalling that July Fourth and all of the other stolen moments that summer. What would Piero tell her if she could talk to him right now? For so many years, he had been her rock and her confidant. There was only one thing she had ever withheld from him—that he would always share her heart with another.

She closed her eyes and let the silence enfold her. Even in the city, she had learned, there was silence. It was not the same as the quiet peacefulness of the vineyard, but it was there. The cacophony of vehicles and sirens and things that go bump in the night became a harmonic chorus of white noise that, when one was used to it, wasn't that different from the chorus of crickets and owls. How she remembered those sounds and the many nights she let them sing her to sleep while her mind whirled with thoughts of Dominic and Piero and the reality that she must choose between them.

The sounds of the city that night were the same, but Marta was not. The situation was not. She no longer had to choose between the two, but it was too late. Dominic's hand on the small of her back as he led her through the center and to the restaurant, along the busy sidewalk, felt the same today as it had thirty-six years before. The way he looked at her, like he could look into her, had not changed. The leaping of her heart and the swirling in her stomach gave her the same thrill now that it had then. But instead of Dominic rivaling Piero for her affections, it was God intervening between Marta and Dominic, continuing to send her the message that they simply were not meant to be.

Marta said a prayer to St. Leo the Great, patron of Little Italy and of the sick. Perhaps he could put in a good word with God. Where Dominic was concerned, Marta wasn't sure she had any credibility with the man upstairs.

7 July 1983

Today, Dominic had to work, but after work, we found just a few minutes to be alone in the last place anyone would look for us. When Paul handed me the note this afternoon, I tucked it into my pocket without reading it or saying anything except thank you. I was trying not to involve my dear friend in more secrecy than necessary.

After telling Zia Isabella that I was running to Angela's to return a shirt I had borrowed, I silently slipped through the wooden doors to St. Leo's. I walked to the pew where I saw the lone figure in the church and properly genuflected before entering. I knelt down and prayed for forgiveness before I sat back in the pew.

Dominic reached over and took my hand in his, and I felt that familiar jolt. For a second, I wondered if God was sending down a bolt of lightning to strike us dead for our sins, but I dismissed the thought. There is a part of me that still hopes that God will see fit to allow us to be together.

For several minutes, we did not speak, and I just let myself feel the contentment of sitting next to Dominic, his hand holding mine. When Dominic leaned over and whispered to me, I was surprised by what he said.

"This church was designed in the late 1800s by a German architect, but the work was done by Italians." He pointed to a statue on the altar. "That's St. John the Evangelist next to Mary. He's the patron saint of love and loyalty, among other things." I felt him glance at me, but I kept my eyes on the statue as though the crucifixion scene was one with which I was not at all familiar and tried not to contemplate love and loyalty.

He continued, "The mural behind the altar is called, St. Leo in Glory. That's St. Leo conversing with God on the cloud. He's the patron of the sick."

"I did not know that I was going to be treated to a church history lesson," I said to him with a smile to show that I did not mind. I asked him how he knew these things.

Dominic shrugged and told me that he was an altar boy for a long time.

I gazed at him, trying to imagine him wearing a black and white cassock and lighting the altar candles. "I bet you were a very good one," I said.

He chuckled. "I don't know about that. Paul was better at it."

"Why do you do that?" I asked, bothered by this constant comparison between the sinful Dominic and the saintly Paul. "Your brother is a fine young man, but he is no better than you."

I saw Dominic's face falter and a pall of sadness cover his eyes. "I wish I was better. I wish I was the man you need me to be." He looked at me and held my gaze as tightly as he held my hand and said, "I wish I could make your aunt and uncle trust me."

"Give them time," I assured him though I am not at all sure that time will help.

Dominic looked at his watch and sighed. I knew that our short time had come to an end.

I squeezed his hand and smiled before I slid across the pew, leaving him alone with his thoughts and God.

"What took you so long? I have been waiting to hear from you all day?"

Marta could hear the sounds of Florence in the background and could almost smell the sweet aroma of pastry in the air and the taste of gelato on her lips. She missed Italy and her friend.

"I thought you would be working, and it is early here."

"Tell me about last night. You went to dinner? How was he? Does he look well?"

Marta laughed. "Slow down! He looks well, very well. He is pale, and his hair is thin, but this I expected after talking to Paul."

"But is he still… the man you knew?"

A sigh escaped her lips. "Allora, he is still the man I knew, only better, I think."

"And you will see him again?"

"Si, today." Marta told Antonella about the center and the little she knew about its founding and what Dominic did there for the boys.

"He sounds…"

"Like a saint? He would scoff at the idea, but si, he has done much good for many people."

"Then go see him. Open your heart to him. See where it takes you."

"Prego. You are a good friend. I would not be here without your love and support."

"You would be there with or without me. It is what is meant to be."

"I pray you are right," Marta said before telling Antonella goodbye. "Ti amo." She disconnected the call and picked up her purse, saying a prayer as she left the house that her friend was right and that her being here was meant to be. Otherwise, she was making a fool of herself over something, perhaps someone, that never was.

"You're back," Tony said with a smile. 'I'm glad. Dom needs a…" He looked at her with a question in his eyes. "A friend."

Marta ignored the implication. "And you're still behind that desk. Are you the resident security guard, Tony?" She smiled. He reminded her of Paul. In fact, now that she was past the anxiety of seeing Dominic and the awe of seeing the center, she took the time to really look at Tony, and yes, he could have been the Paul she knew.

"Not security, though I am studying to be a police officer. Dom knows lots of guys on the force, and he's setting up an internship for me. For now, I just work the front desk."

"Dom must trust you very much." The more she looked at him, the more she saw the many resemblances—the rounded chin, the low brow line, the way he tilted his head when he talked, and his charm and personality. In fact, he looked even more like Paul's daughter, Antonia, and she recalled Paul saying that she had a twin brother.

Tony made a noncommittal sound and shrugged one shoulder. "Trust has to be earned around here, and it's not easy, especially earning Dom's trust. Lucky for me, he's known me since birth."

"You're Paul's son, aren't you?"

"The handsomest, brightest, and most honest," he said with a brilliant smile before leaning over and whispering, "But don't tell my sister that. She thinks she got all the looks and brains between us."

Marta laughed. "You are so much like your father. It's like looking into the past."

"How old were you when you knew my dad and Dom?" His curiosity was piqued.

"About your age, I guess."

"I thought so." He shook his head. "I was sure it was you." He looked at her as appraisingly as she had him. "You're Zia Isa's niece, aren't you?"

She let out a small gasp. "You called her Zia?"

"We all did. My brothers and sisters and me. She was like an older aunt to all of us. She used to talk about you. So did my dad. He said that you and Dom... Well, never mind."

"There you are," Dominic said coming down the hall from his office. "I wondered why you were late. I guess my talkative protégé here has waylaid you."

She looked at Tony, wishing she could learn more. What had they said about her? About her and Dominic?

She smiled and looked back at Dominic. "Tony has been spilling all of the family secrets."

Perhaps she wanted a reaction, or perhaps she was merely pushing open the door, but Dominic just laughed. "We'll be in my office for a bit, Tony, and then we'll be going out for a while."

"No worries, Dom. I'll hold down the fort."

As they walked down the hall, Marta asked, "Why doesn't he call you Uncle Dominic, I mean Uncle Dom?"

"Familiarity breeds contempt," he said, taking a seat on the couch as he had the day before. This time, Marta sat beside him.

"Please, explain."

"I'm just Dom to all the boys. My personal life is personal. My relatives are my business. It just makes things easier that way. If I need to share something personal to make a point or establish a rapport, that's my call. Everyone is safer and more comfortable that way."

"That makes sense. Was Tony a troubled youth? He hardly seems the type." As soon as she said the words, she was sorry. "I didn't mean—"

"No worries. I know what you meant. He's much more like his father than his uncle. No, Tony's never been in trouble. I need someone working out front who I know isn't going to let anyone in he shouldn't and who can keep track of the comings and goings without falling to temptation."

"Without being bribed to withhold information, you mean."

"That and other things, but yeah. He's got my back, and I've got his. That's what family does."

"Speaking of family, it sounds like your family became quite close to my family."

Dominic nodded. "In time, yes. Oh, Paul was always the favorite kid in the neighborhood. It's why your aunt and uncle trusted him so much. I felt bad about that, about what we made him do. He hated being the go-between, you know."

"I always suspected he did, but he never said so to me."

"That's because he was head over heels in love with you, but you knew that. I told you that way back then. I also told you that he knew he didn't have a chance."

"And how did you know that, Dominic? Maybe it was Paul to whom I was attracted."

"Maybe it was," he said before giving her a slow, confident smile. "But I think you liked me from the moment you first saw me watching you from the front step. I know that's when I fell for you."

Marta swallowed, unable to answer. Her face grew hot, and she looked away, but she had made up her mind to do things differently this time. She looked back at Dominic and held his eyes with hers. "Then I suppose it was love at first sight for us both."

She didn't know how he would react or where her words would lead, but she knew they had to be said. After all these years, all the guilt, and all the wondering, she needed him to know that despite her leaving and despite her marrying Piero, she had loved him once. It might be too late now, but she still wanted him to know that their summer together had meant something to her.

Dominic took her hands in his and sat looking at her for a long time before speaking. His words were slow and measured. "I think we should do it right this time. No sneaking around, no relaying messages through my kid brother, no hiding or worrying about who in the neighborhood might see us together. I'd like to take you out. Tonight. On a real date. Will you allow me to do that, Marta? Can we do things the way we should have done them back then?"

There had been too many years, too much time passed, and Marta knew that they couldn't just start over, especially with Dominic being... Then again, she was here, and he was alive, and everything was different. Everything except for the way her body and her heart reacted to him.

"It would be my pleasure to go out with you tonight, Dominic."

10 July 1983

Today, we went downtown to the Inner Harbor. We were at the docks throwing bread to the ducks, and one rather precocious fellow came right up and took a piece out of my hand and nipped my finger. It surprised me so, but Dominic thought it was funny. He just shook his head and laughed.

He said, "He didn't bite you. He just took the bread from you, and your finger got in the way."

I quickly pulled the lens cap from my camera and held it up to my eye, focusing and snapping a photo of him laughing. His dimples were on full display, and his eyes sparkled. When he saw that I'd taken a picture of him, his smile fled. He said, "Why did you do that? What if—"

I cut him off and told him that I didn't care. I said that I wanted a picture of him to remember him by. I couldn't say more. My heart suddenly felt heavy, and tears flooded my eyes.

Dominic rushed to me and took my hand. He led me to a bench, his arms around my shoulders, and pulled me to him. "Mia bella, don't cry."

I looked up at him. "I've never heard you speak Italian," I said through sniffles.

"It's all in there somewhere," he said, pointing to his forehead. "You bring out the best in me, I suppose."

I reached into my bag for a tissue, happy that mamma had taught me always to have one handy. I wiped my eyes and blew my nose. I said to him, "It's not fair. Why can't we see each other? Why must we be secretive? Why can't I have a picture of you?"

It was then that Dominic took a long, deep breath and sighed it out. His eyes became clouded, and a shadow overtook his face. He looked away from me when he spoke.

"Some friends and I—I thought they were friends at the time—we stole a car. We thought it would be fun to take the car and ride through the city, screaming out the windows, playing the music loudly, and acting like we had no cares in the world."

I asked him how old he was at the time, and he told me that he was sixteen and had barely had his license more than a couple months. He was the only one with a license, so he was the one driving the car.

"We weren't drunk, but we'd been drinking. Buzzed with alcohol and the foolishness of our youth, we raced up and down the streets." I listened as he told me the story.

They went from one end of the city to the other in the stolen car, calling out to girls they passed, and revving their engines—he explained this to me—at the stoplights. They thought they were very cool, as he said, and didn't see how anything could go wrong.

They were almost back to Little Italy when a police car pulled out behind them and turned on the lights and siren. Dominic didn't know what to do. He knew he should stop, but the others were yelling for him to keep going, to try to get away from the ensuing car.

Dominic took a corner, as he said, "on two wheels." It was too late to brake when he saw the child running out into the road. He did not know why the little boy was out late at night nor why he ran into the road, but he knew that the car would not stop in time.

Dominic pressed his foot to the brake, and he recalled smelling smoke and rubber, but what he recalled most was the screaming—the boy's mother's and his own.

"The sound haunts me at night, wakes me up when I'm asleep," he told me. He turned to me for the first time and said, "Now, I picture your face, your smile, and my nightmare fades away."

I asked him what happened to the little boy, and his eyes grew sad. "He lived, but he was in bad shape. He had two broken legs, and he still doesn't walk like he should."

"Thank the Lord it was not worse," I said, and he nodded. I asked him what happened next.

"I was arrested and convicted. The other boys all came from a different neighborhood, a different kind of life. While much of my tuition was paid for through charity, their fathers were doctors and lawyers with money to spare. None of them ever made it to court except to testify that it was all my idea—it was not. That I had supplied the alcohol—I had not. And that they wanted me to stop for the officer—they did not."

"So you took the punishment for all of you," I said quietly, and he nodded and squeezed me tighter.

He told me how he had lost everything that night—his place in school, his reputation, the trust of his family, his future, and the desire to live. For five years, he was in a detention center for young men. He got out when he turned twenty-one, and he had been trying to find the will to go on ever since.

"You," he said quietly, looking deeply into my eyes. "You saved my life."

I did not know what to say. He was young and made a bad choice, but he was a good man. I knew it in my soul. But I also knew that I could not be his savior.

I, too, have a choice to make, one that I know will change both of our lives forever no matter how I choose.

Chapter Seven

Marta's entire body tingled with excitement as she dressed, brushed her hair, and applied light makeup. She smiled in the mirror, grateful for good genes that kept her looking younger than her fifty-eight years. Not that it mattered, she thought and smiled. Dominic seemed just as taken with her now as he had when they were both twenty-two.

When the doorbell rang, she practically floated down the stairs to answer it. She recalled that day when she had spied from the top of the stairs, listening to Paul ask Zio Roberto for permission to take her on a tour. Dominic had never had the chance to ring the bell and escort her from the house, and this first official date had her feeling like a young woman again.

When she opened the door, she couldn't even see Dominic for the large bouquet of flowers he held. He peeked around the blossoms and smiled.

"Pinks and purples, right?"

She laughed and took the flowers from him—roses, lavender, larkspur, ranunculus, and carnations filled her senses as she headed toward the kitchen.

"I can't believe you remembered," she called, hearing him on her heels.

When she got to the kitchen, she put down the bouquet and turned to look for a vase, but he caught her arm and pulled her to face him.

"I remember everything. Every small detail, every conversation, the way you looked when you laughed, and the way you looked when you cried. I have kept it all right here." He took her hand and laid it on his heart, and she felt her insides melt away along with the years.

She closed her eyes and breathed. She felt him take a step closer, and she opened her eyes to meet his. She could feel his breath on her face and the rapid pulsing of his heart beneath her hand.

"I remember everything, and I knew that one day, I would see you again, hold you again, and feel my heart come back to life."

Marta wanted him to kiss her, to feel his hands on her, to experience all of the things that they never had a chance to feel or discover. She wanted to close that small step between them, but she did not.

"I've lived a lifetime without you," she said. "I'd like to know what a lifetime with you feels like. I don't want to live it all in one day. I want to know you again, minute by minute, day by day. I want to learn who you were, who you became, and who you are. I want to see life through your eyes and share my eyes' views with you.

Can you give me that? Time to have a life with you? Even if it is just a few days. Is it even possible?"

"I will give you every good moment I have left on this earth, no matter how many or how few they are." He released her hand. "Let's go to dinner. There is much I have to tell you. I don't know what the future holds, but I know that my present is with you."

She nodded, knowing he could not promise what he could not give. For now, dinner would have to be enough.

Dominic drove to a restaurant outside of the city. Marta stole glances of him as often as possible, trying to assess his well-being. She was looking forward to dinner, but she was anxious about what he was going to tell her.

When they arrived at the restaurant, Dominic told her to wait while he walked around and opened the door for her—always the gentleman. He walked her to the front door, his hand in its familiar position on her lower back, and she felt as though no time had passed at all since he had walked her through the streets of Baltimore in their youth. They were led to an intimate table in the back of the restaurant just as they had been the previous night, but tonight felt different, more formal, more like a real date though she could scarcely count the years since her last real date, pre-marriage, and it suddenly occurred to her that it had been here with him.

"Did we…?" she asked, looking around.

"We did. It was the only night we actually went out to dinner together. I thought you might have forgotten."

How could she have forgotten? It was the night of the kiss, the night she knew she had let things go too far. It was also the best night of her entire summer.

"I remember it well," she said with a smile. "I can't believe this place is still in business."

"Technically, it's not. The restaurant that we went to was here, but it has changed hands and names many times since then. I find that the food always remains good."

They ordered a bottle of wine, Dominic deferring to Marta to pick it out, as well as an appetizer. Marta was concerned about him drinking, but he assured her that his doctor had approved alcohol in moderation as long as it didn't make him feel sick.

Dominic was quieter than he had been, and Marta tried to wait patiently to get past the idle chit chat and hear what he had promised to tell her.

While they were eating their meal—steak for Dominic and chicken for Marta, both with healthy servings of vegetables and rice—Dominic swallowed a bite, took a deep breath, and laid down his fork.

"I suppose there's no use putting it off any longer."

Marta saw the worry in his eyes and wondered if he thought this would be the last time they saw each other, once she knew the full extent of his illness. That led her to wonder if he was right. After all, she had a life back home, a job, a child and grandchildren. What was here other than an unrequited love with a dying man? She immediately chastised herself for the callous thought and gave Dominic her full attention.

"I'm ready. Please, tell me."

"I'm sure it comes as no surprise that Paul and I took up smoking after you left. It wasn't new to me. I'd smoked in the juvenile home when I could get away with it, but I quit when I returned home. The craving never went away, and eventually Paul and I, like most of our friends, gave into the habit. Paul, as always, was much wiser than I was though. He quit after about six or seven years at Sophia's urging. She never liked the nasty habit, but she tolerated it outdoors until they had kids. Paul quit cold turkey and never went back."

"I take it you kept smoking though." Marta took a long sip of wine, leaving her food barely touched.

Dominic nodded. "I knew it was a death sentence, but to be honest, I didn't care."

A chill went through her, and she felt a lump form in her throat.

"I was still struggling at the time, trying to find my place, going from job to job, without any focus in my life." He paused and took a drink, a faraway look settled in his eyes for a moment before he continued. "Then Sally walked into the restaurant one day. Paul had recently opened the place, and I was helping out, in between jobs once again. Anyway, Sally had a proposition for me.

"He had a client, a nineteen-year-old kid, who was going to be sent to prison for stealing a car unless Sally could prove that the kid could be a productive member of society. The judge was a new breed around here, one who believed that kids who made mistakes should be given a second chance. She thought this kid deserved the chance to right his wrong, but he couldn't go back home. Things were bad there, and he'd never have the support he needed. Sally wanted me to take him in, to mentor him, and help him find his way."

"Yet you hadn't found yours," Marta commented.

Dominic chuckled. "Sally's known me my whole life. He knew what I needed when I didn't know myself. He went to Father Sebastian, and they talked me into it and helped me find a house that I could afford—I'd been living in the one-room apartment above the restaurant. Sally gave me a loan for the down payment amidst my protests. He and Father even helped me find a job working at the soap factory. Proctor and Gamble closed it a couple years later, but by then, I had a new vision for my life, was going to college at night to study social work, and Sally and I opened the center."

"You'd found your way."

"I had, and so had that kid, Marcos. He got himself cleaned up, went to Morgan State University, and is now an attorney working with youth who get into trouble. Many of our kids come through him."

Marta was glad to have Dominic fill in the blanks from their previous conversations about his past, but she was anxious for him to get to the present.

"So, you got a new lease on life and a new purpose, but you kept smoking."

He gave her a wry smile that told her that he understood what she was asking. "Yeah, for about twenty years. It was the kids who got me to stop.

Smoking was forbidden in the center. Sally insisted on it, and I knew it wasn't a healthy choice. I just couldn't make myself quit." He finished off his broccoli and refilled his glass of wine and hers. "I told you that we make the kids go to church."

"You did." Marta took a drink of her wine and waited for him to continue.

"One Sunday, we were leaving Mass, and the kids started talking about what they were giving up for Lent. This one kid, Denzel, he looked at me and said, 'Dom's giving up smoking.' Just like that. It wasn't even a question."

"And you did?"

He nodded. "I did." He took a long drink before he said, "But it was too late."

Dominic told Marta that his lungs were already in the pre-cancerous stage at that point, and over the next several years, the disease took hold without his knowledge. By the time he had symptoms, his lungs were in pretty bad shape, as he put it.

"Is it stage 4?" she asked, her voice trembling.

"It may as well be," Dominic answered, avoiding her eyes. "It's classified as 3b. Inoperable. It's in both lungs, multiple tumors."

"Are you being treated?"

Dominic shrugged. "Yeah, but it's all experimental and not aimed at saving my life, just pro-longing it. To be truthful, if it were just me, I'd stop the treatments, but I've got the kids. They need me. And now…" He looked at her and smiled a sad smile. "Well, I don't know. Maybe I need to think in broader terms."

Marta felt as though she were twenty-two again, hearing the unspoken plea, his desire for her to stay, to be part of his life, to try to make things work. She closed her eyes and breathed deeply.

"Dominic," she began.

"Stop," he said. "I'm not asking for anything. Just seeing you again, just knowing that you're happy and that you had a good life. That's enough to make me want to keep living. Even if it's from a distance, to know that you can be a small part of my life, makes life worth living."

She wasn't ready to commit to anything, so she asked. "Where are you with the treatments?"

He sat back and sighed. "I just started chemo. If my body tolerates it, and the doctors say it should, I'll move on to immunotherapy with Imfinzi when the chemo is done. That can be done for up to a year. After that..." he shrugged. "It's in God's hands."

"What are your chances of survival?" She hated to ask, but this was where they were, and he didn't seem to mind talking about it.

"Depends. The treatment may or may not work, and there are possible side effects that could mean stopping treatment or could lead to other life-threatening issues." He leaned back toward her and placed his arms on the table. "The bottom line is, I don't know. The doctors don't know. A lot of this is trial and error. I could live another two or three years or be gone next week. I know that's harsh, but I wanted you to know. I won't pressure you. I won't ask you to stay or give up your life. I don't know what I'm facing, and I don't want you to feel like you need to be here. I'm a big boy. I've got a good support system—Paul and Soph and their kids, Sally and Millie, Father Sebastian and my Church family, and the boys at the center. You don't need to feel guilty or responsible or like you need to be involved. This, us seeing each other again, being here tonight, all of it, is a gift, one I will be forever grateful for, and I don't need more than that. I'm content with my life and the man I've become. Seeing you again just makes whatever happens a little bit better."

He'd given her an out. He'd said she didn't need to feel guilty or responsible, or be involved, but she did. She felt guilty and responsible, and she thought she wanted to be involved, somehow, in some way. Perhaps if she hadn't left, his life would have turned out differently. Then again, so might the lives of all the boys he had helped over the years. Just as she would never have had Nicola, the boys would never have had Dominic.

"I'm not sure what to say," Marta told him honestly.

"Say nothing. We're together for now. That's all that matters." He hesitated before he asked, "How long will you be here?"

"I have another meeting tomorrow in Washington. It that goes well, I begin my vacation. I am due back at Uffizi in two and a half weeks." Her own words pained her as much as the expression on his face. What had seemed like such a long trip when she first left Italy now felt like a brief moment.

"Then we have two and a half weeks to continue seeing each other."

"It's not enough," she blurted without thinking.

"It will have to be, my love, but I warn you, it will not be an easy couple of weeks for me. I have my next treatment on Monday."

"And I will be at your side," she said hastily. For the decision had been made. She would spend the time she had here with him. She would not abandon him again, at least not until she was forced to, but she would not think about that now.

"No," he said firmly. "I've thought a lot about it since we left Isa's house, and it wasn't fair of me to say the things I did, to talk about a lifetime together. I won't ask that of you. I'll go for chemo and then call you in a few days, when I'm feeling up to it, and we can see each other. I don't want you to be my nursemaid, holding my hand while I sit on the bathroom floor."

"I want to share a lifetime. That's what we promised earlier—a lifetime in whatever time we have left. Doesn't that mean in good times and bad, in sickness and in health?"

Dominic gave a sad laugh. "Oh, my dearest Marta, if only those vows had been made years ago, then maybe that would be so, but you and I had different paths to follow. I admit, I was resentful at the time. After a while anyway, when I realized you weren't coming back, when Isa broke the news to me that you had, in fact, gotten married. I was angry and said I was glad you left and other things that would be too hurtful to us both for me to repeat."

Her heart broke at his words, but she could not blame him.

"But I moved on, albeit not on a straight and narrow road. You and I made the best of what we'd been given and what we'd chosen. Looking back, I have no regrets, and I know that you don't either. When you speak of your son, even your husband, I see and hear the love you have for them both. I love my work and my boys, and though it's not the same, it's okay. I want you in my life but not to hold my hand and watch me suffer and die. We'll do what we can while you're here, spend time together and make up for all the lost years as much as we can, but then you will return home to your family, and I will live out my life as God wills it."

Marta tried to take it all in—his words, his wishes, his plan to just send her home and say goodbye, probably for forever, and his underlying faith.

"You've changed," she said quietly. "You smile and laugh more easily. You talk openly about God, not just in church. Even facing…" She could not say the word. "Even facing the unknown, you seem…accepting."

"What choice do I have? I can fight and work hard to overcome the odds, but in the end, my life is not my own. It belongs to God. Once I figured that out, everything else just fell into place. The same will happen with this disease." He looked at her and smiled. "And with us." He reached across the table and took her hand.

"Now, tell me more about you. Do you still take pictures?"

15 July 1983

I confess, I have sinned. I allowed Dominic to take me on a date. I pretended that there was no Piero, and I let things go too far.

Angela and I were playing tennis when Dominic was suddenly there, watching us, cheering me on. When we finished, Angela said she had to go and left me alone with her cousin. It was the first time we had seen each other since the day he told me of his arrest. He has been working many hours at an automobile repair shop, and he hates it, but he says it is the only place that would hire him. But today is Saturday, and the shop closed at noon, so he came looking for me.

"I want to take you to dinner," he said, and I found myself smiling and nodding yes before I even thought about what it meant.

I went home and showered and changed into a summer dress I bought on a shopping trip with Angela. I told Zia Isabella yet another lie, that Angela and I were going to have dinner together. Zia Isabella approves of Angela, and she is becoming my alibi more than Paul though Paul continues to be a good friend to me. When I was dressed, I walked down toward Angela's house but, with a quick look to be sure nobody was watching, I headed to the station by the Shot Tower. Dominic was waiting in a borrowed car on the corner.

He told me not to worry, that the car belongs to his father and that he said Dominic could borrow it for the night. His face reddened and he looked away when he said, "He says he's trying to trust me again."

My heart broke for him, but my mind cautioned me that we were sneaking around, hiding from watchful eyes, and lying to those we loved, those who thought we could be trusted.

"Does he know about me?" I asked hesitantly.

He answered, "He knows there is a girl, a woman," he corrected. "I told him that I'm not ready to share details, and Paul assured him that she, you, could be trusted to keep me out of trouble." He grinned as he opened the door for me, and I felt slightly better though I questioned whether either of us was truly out of trouble.

We drove out of the city to a restaurant that Dominic said he'd heard about but had never been to. He knew his way around quite well and only consulted a map once. When we arrived, he walked me inside with his hand on my back, and my body reacted to his touch with shockwaves of pleasure. We were taken to a table in the back and given menus.

Dominic asked if I would like wine, and I said yes, but he ordered only Coca-Cola. I had yet to see him drink, and I asked him about it. He told me that he was not drinking while he was on parole. He could, but he thought it best not to since it was part of what had gotten him into trouble to begin with. I changed my mind and ordered a Coca-Cola, too.

I can't ever remember talking as much as I did over that meal. Dominic asked question after question, delighting in my tales of growing up at Belle Uve and my adventures at university. He told me that he hopes to go to college someday, but he does not know if that will be possible. He does not know what he wants to do with his life or what kinds of opportunities are still available to him.

He told me about his Nonno who no longer remembers who anyone is. That makes me so sad. That is why he and Paul have so much responsibility in the house. With their parents working, they must help their Nonna care for their Nonno. I am reminded of Zia Isabella's mention of caring for Zio Roberto when he came home from war and how mi nonno cared for mi nonna when she could no longer walk because of joint pain. It is what we do for those we love. I can't help but wonder how I will be called on to help a loved one someday.

Over dinner, Dominic and I talked and laughed and shared hopes and dreams, but somehow, none of the dreams I shared involved Piero, not directly. I talked about the job I would have when I returned home and how I hoped to have a family someday, but I never mentioned my upcoming marriage. It was wrong, and I know it, but it did not feel right, bringing Piero into the conversation, into my life with Dominic.

When dinner was over, we drove to a place with a small pier that Dominic said was for fishing. Halfway to the pier, he stopped the car and looked over at me and asked, "Do you want to drive?"

I had told him that I had never driven a car on the highway, only around the vineyard. I do not have a car of my own, and I do not need one in Firenze. I do not even have my license. Dominic was shocked by this and said that in the United States, everyone rushes to get their license on the day they turn sixteen. It is a rite of passage, he said.

My hands tingled as I placed them on the wheel, but Dominic was there to guide me, and before long, driving felt as normal as walking. I drove us all the way to the pier, feeling a sense of freedom I do not think I have ever felt.

It was late when we got there, but the moon was full, and stars dotted the sky. We sat on the edge of the dock, holding hands, and looking at the stars like we did the night we went skating. We spoke little, enjoying the gentle sway of the dock and found contentment in the comfortable silence.

When Dominic turned to me, I felt my heart leap and my breathing quicken. He whispered my name, "Marta." And that was all it took. I leaned toward him and met his lips with mine. His hand slid around my neck and into my hair, and our kisses grew hungry as my arms found their way around his neck. He laid me back onto the dock, and my stomach filled with butterflies. All thoughts left my mind, and I let him kiss me, and I kissed him back, for a very long time.

I kept my eyes closed when I felt him pull back, not wanting the kissing to end. I felt the weight of him leave me, and I opened my eyes to find him sitting up, looking out over the water.

I sat up and asked him what was wrong. He smiled and took my hand and said, "Nothing is wrong. Everything is right, and that is the problem."

I told him that I did not understand, and he said, "The summer will soon come to an end. You're leaving in a few weeks, and I don't know if I'll ever see you again."

I could not offer any assurances. I knew that he was right. I would return home in three weeks. My parents expected me to return, and there was Piero. I finally allowed him to enter my mind, to become a part of this night.

Piero is a good man, a wonderful man, a man who loves me and has our future well-planned. We will be married, and he will teach while I work at museum and take pictures. He has worked hard to save money and told me in his last letter that he has put the down payment on a house. We will live in Fiesole, a small town above Florence, and we will take the train into the city together every day to go to work. Our children will go to school in the town, and we will go to church and live a happy life together. Piero is so happy, so anxious for me to return home. How can I betray him? How could I have betrayed him with Dominic, a man so different from him?

I remained silent, lost in thought, and after a few moments, Dominic began to stand and pulled me up with him. He laid his hands gently on each side of my face and looked into my eyes. He said, "You have changed my life, Marta. You have shown me that I can be better, that I am still a good man. Somehow, I will make others see this, too. I'm going to work to make the world see me the way you do. And I will find you. I am asking you to stay, begging you to stay, but if you have to go, then someday, I will find you and love you the way you should be loved."

His words made my heart soar and break at the same time. When he leaned in to kiss me, I kissed him back, but the hunger was gone. I knew that the woman he loved was not who he thought she was. She is a liar and a betrayer and a cheater.

I know now that while I was saving Dominic, I was condemning myself.

Chapter Eight

Dominic asked if he could accompany Marta to Washington, and she happily accepted his offer to drive them into the city. After her meeting, at which all of the terms were agreed upon and contracts signed, Marta led Dominic through some of her favorite exhibits in the museum.

"You come alive when you talk about the paintings and the artists. It's like you can see into their souls and know what they were attempting to portray."

She blushed at his words but did not know why. Perhaps it was because this statement felt intimate in a way, like he could read her mind and her soul. She supposed that should not surprise her. It had always been so with Dominic. "I've learned a lot over the years," she said, trying to dismiss her passion as nothing other than her education, but he saw through her.

"No," he said, stopping and facing her. "It's not what you've learned that comes out when you talk about paintings or photography or other works of art. It's a passion that comes from deep within. I can see it, hear it, and feel it. You are most you when you're in a museum, just as you are when your eye is to a lens and your finger is on the button."

"The shutter," she said as her body filled with warmth. "It's not called a button. It's a shutter. And how do you do that? How do you look inside of me and see what I feel? After all these years, how do you know me as if it were yesterday?"

He cupped her chin with his hand. "Because you have lived inside my heart for all this time."

Aware that they were not the only visitors to the museum, Marta took his hand from her chin and held it tightly in her hand and led him to the next room. His love overwhelmed her, as it had back then, and she didn't know how to contain her emotions. She fought back tears, not even knowing why they came.

They left the museum, added more quarters to the meter, and strolled down the National Mall. It was hot and humid, and Marta felt sweat sliding down her back. She was glad she had changed her shoes when they were at the car but wished she had on shorts and a t-shirt like most of the other people they passed. Dominic, dressed in khaki pants and a short-sleeved button-down shirt, took a handkerchief from his pocket and wiped his forehead. Upon close inspection, she saw that he was pale and that beads of perspiration formed a line above his top lip. He did not look well, and she began maneuvering him to a nearby bench.

"Why did you not tell me that you aren't feeling well?"

"I'm fine. It's just a little hot, that's all."

She reached up and felt his forehead. "You're burning up."

"We all are. It's ninety degrees out here." He smiled, but she could tell that it was forced.

"Let's go. I'm taking you home."

"You can't drive. You don't have a license."

"Of course, I do. Come on." She didn't have an American license, but she was no longer twenty-two, and a car was sometimes a necessity, especially when she wanted to go home to her family. It was not the same as driving on what Dominic called The Beltway, but she had driven in Rome, and if she could drive there, she could drive anywhere.

By the time they reached the car, he was leaning on her, and she could feel his breathing becoming shallow. He was asleep when they turned off of the beltway, and Marta lessened her grip on the wheel, glad to be on a less crowded road, and the blood returned to her fingers. She reached for her phone and called Paul, apprising him of the situation.

"Take him straight to Johns Hopkins. I'll meet you there." She pulled over while he gave her the address, then she did her best to focus on the road as she followed the mechanical voice giving her directions to the hospital. Paul called back a little while later and told her where to park. He was waiting for her when she pulled into the space in the garage. He already had a wheelchair waiting. Dominic was awake but incoherent, his eyes going back and forth between Marta and his brother, his breath steady but weak.

"I'm so sorry. I didn't know he wasn't feeling well. I would never have let him go!"

"Marta, it's not your fault. You know Dom. He does what he wants."

She nodded, still feeling guilty, and followed Paul through the automatic doors. They made their way through security and into the ER. The nurse took Dominic back as soon as Paul wheeled him through the door, and there was nothing for them to do but wait.

Marta's nerves were on edge, and she wrung her hands with despair as they sat in the waiting room. They had only just found each other again. Was this to be the end?

"Ever heard of St. Dominic Savio?" Paul asked, breaking into her dark thoughts. She turned toward him.

"I've heard of him. Why?"

"Do you know anything about him?"

Marta shook her head. "No, I don't believe so. Just that he is not the same Dominic who founded a monastery in Firenze."

"No, he's not. As a boy and teenager, Dominic Savio volunteered at a home for young boys. He taught them about God and taught his faith by example. He helped those boys become men even though he was just a boy himself. He died at the age of 14 of a lung disease."

Marta was quiet for a moment, taking in Paul's words. "What an amazing coincidence," she finally said.

"No such thing, Marta."

"What do you mean?" She looked at him with interest.

"There's no such thing as coincidence. Everything that happens is part of God's plan. We might not see it at the time, but with hindsight, we can look back and see that God's plan is always perfect. He puts us where we need to be, with the people we need to be with, and in the circumstances we need to be in. We make our own choices, but he leads us to the crossroads and then carries us on the journey."

"You believe Dominic was meant to end up where he is, helping the boys at the center."

"He was born to do it. Not only because of his namesake, but because he has the heart and the mind and the will to put others first. You know that firsthand."

Marta blinked. "Me? What do you mean?"

Paul's smile was sad. "He loved you more than anyone he's ever loved. I know he still does. But he knew that you had to make your own decisions and choose the life that was best for you. He knew he couldn't provide for you, for a family, that he was in an uphill battle at that point in his life. He wanted you to stay. He wanted you to be part of his life forever, but he also wanted you to be happy and have a full life. He wanted you to be happy in Italy and feel love and have a happy marriage with kids even though it broke his heart every time he thought about it. He never gave up on seeing you again someday, and he was confident that God would allow it to happen. He was content to wait and let God's plan unfold. I think, when he was diagnosed, he had a feeling you would be back before the end."

"I broke his heart when I told him goodbye."

"Yes, but he could've tried to stop you. Deep down, he knew it would've been wrong."

"Why didn't he ever look for me?"

"Once he knew you'd gotten married, he accepted that as part of the plan. He would never have come between you and your husband. I think you know that."

"I would not have let him," she said, knowing it was true.

"I believe that, and so did he, but he knew it would be painful for all of you, so he worked hard to find his place and make his peace with himself, his family, his neighbors, and God. When Sally offered him a chance to redeem those boys, it was the chance he'd been waiting for to redeem himself. It didn't take away the pain from losing you, but it did give him the renewal of life he so desperately needed."

She asked the question that had nagged at her ever since she had learned of all of Dominic's work with the center. "Why could I not find mention of him online? Not in the papers or Facebook or anywhere? Surely, he's been recognized for his work."

Paul nodded. "He has. He's gotten many awards from the diocese, the city, and even a national one, but he won't appear in public to accept them, and he won't do interviews. He asks that his name be kept out of any stories about the center, and he prefers there not be stories about the center. He says it's for the sakes of the boys."

"Why do you think it is?" she asked, catching the implication in his words.

"I think he still doesn't believe he's a good person deserving of the accolades. He still sees himself as the kid who screwed up. I think it's partly because he believes that his screw-up cost him the love of his life"

She felt the sting of his words but knew that he didn't mean to hurt her. "Has he found any happiness in all these years? True happiness?"

"Yes, Marta, he's been happy. The boys bring out the best in him, just like you did back then. It was meeting you that put him on the right path, and I believe that being with you again will help lead him on his final path home."

"I loved my husband very much, but I never stopped loving Dominic. Sometimes, memories of him would float, unexpectedly, into my mind, and I would hold onto them. I didn't know if I would ever see him again, but I never stopped wishing for the best for him."

"I can say the same for Dom," Paul said. "After a while, he stopped talking about you, stopped telling me that he was going to find you someday, but I know the thought was always there. He never let any of us see his pain or sense his feeling of loss, but I know that he longed for you through all of these years."

Marta nodded, but couldn't speak. Perhaps Paul had not seen Dominic's pain, but she had. She had seen his pain and had felt his loss. She had not only witnessed his tears; she had been the cause of them.

A short time later, they were allowed into the room where Dominic had been seen by his doctor. He smiled when they entered. "I thought I'd add a little excitement to the day."

"Are you all right?" Marta asked, resisting the urge to rush to his side and take his hand.

"I'm fine. Just a reaction to the disease and the treatments. I guess I need more rest than I realized."

"No surprise there," Paul said. "You never listen to anyone when they try to tell you what to do, even your doctors."

Marta knew that wasn't true, but she didn't argue. Dominic could not have accomplished all he had if he hadn't taken the advice of Sally or Father Sebastian, but she supposed that siblings always saw each other differently than the rest of the world did.

"When can you go home?" Paul asked.

"As soon as the doctor signs off. Like I said, I'm fine. No need to worry."

This was the Dominic she knew, the man she'd seen glimpses of back then—the one who trusted in the future, not the one who scowled and barked orders and acted like he was angry with the world. Dominic was a different man with her, and she knew it. He opened up to her, allowed her to see his vulnerable yet hopeful side, and made her feel like the world was theirs. She suspected it was the man the boys at the center saw as well. These days, that might be the man he showed to the world. She honestly couldn't say yet.

While they waited for Dominic to be released, the three of them reminisced about the past, and Marta remembered how easily she had fallen into friendship with them and with their cousin.

"Where is Angela now? I'd love to see her."

Paul and Dominic exchanged a look, and Marta felt her blood grow cold.

Paul answered, "Angela and William got married and had kids. They moved to New York when William got a job working at Morgan Stanley—an investment firm in the city. When the kids went to school, Angela took a job as a receptionist at one of the businesses at the top of One World Trade Center."

The room grew quiet. Marta knew the rest of the story without Paul needing to recount it. Tears sprang to her eyes. "Was she... Did they?"

Paul shook his head. "Her name's engraved on the Memorial. That's about all that remains."

Marta thought about the vibrant young woman with the bright red lipstick and infectious laugh. She could play a mean game of tennis, and she loved to roller skate and go to the movies and craved adventure. It didn't feel real to think that she was gone, her life taken in an instant. Marta sniffled and rubbed the back of her hand across her cheek to wipe away a tear.

"But she got to marry William," she said quietly. "Her family accepted him?"

"Eventually," Paul said. "He had to prove himself, but he did."

Marta looked over at Dominic, recalling how he told her how he proved himself to Zia Isabella only to discover that Marta had married someone else. His eyes held sadness, but he smiled. "They had a good life together," he said. "William was a good man who took care of Angela and the kids."

"Where are they now? William and the children?"

"William is back here. He transferred to the Baltimore office and moved back home afterward." She saw Dominic swallow before he continued. "He needed help with the kids—they were still young—so he moved back home so that his parents could help. Zia Rosa was happy to have the kids nearby even if it meant they were being raised in the old Irish neighborhood." Dominic laughed. "They're grown now, but they still live in Maryland." He glanced at Paul before continuing. "Um, Jack and Marta are both married and have kids of their own."

Marta's heart caught in her throat. "Marta?" She felt her own name in a whisper on her lips.

"She always thought of you," Paul said, "and admired the way you came here that summer, leaving your family and friends behind. She thought of you as strong and confident, and she wanted the same for her daughter."

Marta remembered being anything but strong and confident. It was funny; she always attributed those qualities to Angela.

"We wrote for a short time, but…" Marta remembered how guilty she felt, how her letters to Angela had lessened after she married Piero. She wasn't able to live in both worlds at the same time, and it became harder and harder to separate them each time she received a letter and heard that Dominic was going out with this girl or that. Despite his admission that he had never found the right one after her, Angela had made it seem as though he had moved on. Perhaps that had been for the best.

"I always thought of her as a good friend," Marta said now, wishing she had kept in touch with the woman who had kept her secret all those weeks and had helped her hide her comings and goings.

A nurse appeared with papers for Dominic to sign, and then the three of them left together with Paul driving Dominic's car, explaining to his brother that he had taken the metro downtown rather than worrying about how to get both cars back home. They rode in silence, Dominic's illness and the news of Angela's untimely death riding with them, taking up all of the air and space inside the vehicle.

20 July 1983

Angela came by today and tried to get me to leave the house. I have not wanted to go anywhere or see anyone, and Zia Isabella is worried that I am ill. I told her that I am suffering from homesickness, but I am suffering from the loss of Dominic. For how can I see him now? How can I look into his eyes knowing that I have kept the truth from him? How can I return to Piero with thoughts of Dominic in my mind and my heart? How can I ever wash away the taste of his kisses or brush off the feel of his hands in my hands, on my waist, or tangled in my hair? How can I tell him that I cannot do as he wishes and stay? That is the real question, for if I see him again, I fear that I will not be able to tell him no.

I came to America for an adventure, and God has provided, but it was an adventure for which I was not prepared. What message is he sending me? How could he have brought Dominic into my life only to remind me constantly that it cannot be?

I leave in little more than two weeks' time, and I know that I must see him again. I must tell him goodbye. I must convince myself that there is nothing there, that my life is with Piero, but I fear that seeing him again will unleash all of the feelings I have for him and the longing to stay here and be with him forever. For that is what I want—to stay, to be with Dominic. If I see him again, I know I will not have the strength to say goodbye.

Dear God, please release me from this pain and guilt. Please help me to find the will to tell Dominic goodbye. I know that we are not meant to be, but I cannot imagine my life without him. I am caught in a trap from which I cannot find release. Please help me to do and say the right things so that our lives will follow your will. And help me to believe, no matter what happens, that I have chosen the right path.

The entire family was gathered at Paul and Sophia's house in Little Italy. It was larger than the house he and Dominic had grown up in as well as Zia Isa's house, but with Paul and Sophia, all five of their children, three spouses, and three grandchildren, the house felt very small. Marta stood in a corner looking around at all the familiar faces, for the resemblance to their parents and their uncle ran through all of them, and she found herself missing her family more than she realized.

"Is everything okay?" Dominic asked, slipping his arm around her.

"Si. It is difficult to be away from Nicola and the children for so long. Even when I am in Firenze, I know that I can see them in just a couple hours if I want to."

Dominic looked down at the Coca-Cola in his hand, swirled the liquid around the small blocks of ice, and looked back at Marta. "You don't have to stay, you know. You can go back. I wouldn't hold it against you. Not like last time." He gave her a lopsided grin that melted her heart.

"I will go back when I am ready. Until then, a lifetime, remember?" She gave him a loving smile and reminded herself not to think about how short that lifetime would be.

"Dom, Marta, come on over. I got something to show you." Paul called to them across the room, waving for them to go to him. He stood by a bookcase on the opposite wall. When they neared, he pulled a photo album from one of the shelves. He flipped through the pages until he came to a stop and turned the book to face them. "Ain't this a blast from the past?"

Marta reached for the book without even realizing she had done so. She was mesmerized by the picture taken at a local swimming pool. She and Angela sat on the side of the pool with their legs dangling in the water, smiling broadly, their olive skin shining in the sunlight, no doubt slathered with baby oil. From the water, Paul waved and Dominic grinned, and Marta recalled how his scowl had slowly been replaced by a deepening smile as the summer went by. He changed from a brooding, frowning stranger with a gruff voice and short temper to a kind-hearted gentleman with a beautiful laugh and twinkling eyes.

"Who took that?" She asked, not remembering posing for it at all.

"I think William did. It was my camera. That I remember. We were quite the crew, huh? I was just a kid, you were just coming back to us, Dom. William was so much older, Angela was the prettiest girl in town—"

"Hey, hey, present company excluded, right?" Dominic spoke up, playfully punching his brother in the arm.

"Of course." Paul winked at Marta. "We all know you were the real looker," he said to Dominic which elicited another punch, this one a little harder. "I'm kidding. Marta was the exotic one."

"Me?" She stifled a laugh. "I don't think I've ever been called exotic."

"Oh, come on. You were the unknown, the mysterious one who dropped out of the sky one day and became one of us. We were all trying to figure you out all summer."

"I don't think I was that mysterious," she said quietly while remembering how she had kept so much to herself—her engagement for one thing. Keeping that secret meant that there were many other small details of her life she wasn't able to share. Had they been able to sense that, feel that she was always holding back, being elusive?

"All women are mysteries to Paul," Sophia said with a roll of her eyes. "Don't listen to a word he says. Dinner's ready. Come on into the dining room."

Marta handed the album back to Paul and watched him place it between several other volumes.

"Were these all your mother's?"

"They were. She loved pictures. She wasn't great at taking them, but she loved it when people gave them to her. She spent hours putting these books together so that we'd always have these reminders of the past."

She heard a tinge of pain in his voice. "You miss her."

Paul shrugged. "Doesn't everyone miss their mother after she's gone?"

"Dominic told me that there was an accident."

"Yeah, on the beltway. At least it was quick for them both. Hard for the rest of us, but over in an instant for them."

"I'm so sorry, Paul." She laid her hand gently on his arm.

He shrugged. "We had them for as long as God allowed, and I still have many good memories."

Marta thought of her daughter-in-law, Alexandra, and all the years she and her mother were estranged. Thankfully, they had reconciled, but Alexandra had grieved her loss for so long before she was able to break through her mother's walls, built after the deaths of her husband and son.

Marta thought of her own mother and how she regretted that her mamma had never seen Nicola's children. Her parents had been so much older when they met and even older when she was born. Marta was their one shot, and because of that, she became their whole

world, but they were always very different from the
parents of her friends. They were almost a generation
above them, so they didn't do many of the things other
families did together. And there was always the vineyard
that kept them busy all the time.

"I am happy you have those memories. Mi mamma
was very special, and I do miss her, but she and I did not
have the same relationship that you and your mamma
had. She was older, more like a grandmother to me.
Actually, I think she was more of a mother to Nicola
than to me. I think his love of the vineyard gave him and
my parents a bond that I could not share."

"I never knew that," Dominic said. "I always
assumed that you and your parents were close."

"We were, but it was different, hard to explain. Then
after that summer..." She looked at him wistfully.
"Things weren't quite the same between me and papà
for a long time. Not until Nicola was born."

Marta was pensive through the meal and for the rest
of the evening after that. She loved her parents dearly,
but she wasn't sure that she ever looked at them the way
Paul's children looked at him and Sophia, that she ever
laughed with them the way the D'Angelos laughed so
easily with each other. She wondered if her parents had
even realized how different their relationship was
compared to other families.

"Something upset you tonight," Dominic said when
he walked her to her door. She hadn't said a word on the
short ride home, her thoughts still on her own childhood

and the event that caused a deep rupture in her relationship with her father.

"I don't think I was a very good daughter," she said quietly.

"What do you mean?"

She shook her head. "I don't think I ever took the time to get to know my parents, or anyone in my family, even Zia Isabella. I spent my entire life taking photographs, but I don't think we ever had a single, family album. Your mother had so many."

Dominic took her elbow and stopped her, turning her to him. "Not all families are like ours, and pictures can be deceiving. My relationship with my parents was rocky at best. After my lapse in judgment, my father barely looked at me. When he did, his eyes were full of disappointment. And my mother, she had this notion that both of her sons would grow up to be saints. I certainly shattered that belief."

Marta smiled. "I don't know about that. I think you're doing pretty well in the saint department."

"Nothing is as it seems, Marta. You know that better than anyone. Not all families or all relationships are perfect. We take what we've been given, and we work to make the most of it. In the end, as long as we all loved each other, that's all that matters. Not every day has to be a kodak moment for it to all be good."

"You are a very wise man, Dominic D'Angelo."

He took her hand and led her up the steps to the front door. "I like the way I look in your eyes."

They stopped on the top step, and he ran his finger down her cheek. "Goodnight, Marta. Sweet dreams." He pressed a short, chaste kiss to her lips and waited for her to unlock the door and go inside.

Marta turned back to Dominic. "Goodnight, Dominic. Thank you for tonight."

She watched him leave and thought about the boy she knew and the man she was coming to know. Just like when they were young, she found him so easy to talk to. She hadn't thought that possible at first, but once he opened up to her, she found that she could talk to him about almost anything. That hadn't changed. It made her wonder what might have happened had she been completely truthful with him back then. Would they have stayed together? Would they have this easy, comfortable relationship they have now? Would they have been good parents?

She felt guilty for wondering, but she couldn't help herself. Piero had been a wonderful father, but he had never hidden his disappointment in Nicola for his choosing the vineyard over what Piero saw as more noble careers. Would Dominic, because of his own past, have been more willing to let Nicola make his own decisions?

She sighed and shook the thoughts from her head. Families were complicated, but Dominic was right. Everyone is given the family they are given, and they must all make the decision to love each other, flaws and all, especially during those non-kodak moments.

Chapter Nine

The camera flashed over and over as Marta took pictures of the young men at play. She asked permission beforehand, assuring all of them that the photos would be for private use only. Some of the young men agreed while others asked her to leave them out, and she obliged their wishes.

When she had arrived at the center early that morning, it was Dominic who met her at the door, but she almost didn't recognize him. He was completely bald, and she was stunned at the sight of him without his beautiful, dark wavy hair. He smiled and rubbed his hand over his head.

"I guess I should've warned you. I had Tony help me this morning. I woke up on a pillow of hair and decided I was going to take matters into my own hands, so to speak. I couldn't get it all, but Tony says he thinks he did a pretty good job with the back." He turned his head so that she could see all of it.

Marta stood with her mouth agape for a moment before composing herself. She smiled genuinely and said, "I love it. You're even more handsome than you already were. The spitting image of Sean Connery."

Dominic laughed and said in a thick brogue, "Aye, because I have so much Scottish blood running through these Italian veins."

She laughed and took his offered arm. Whether he had hair or not, he was still the same Dominic, and she realized with each passing moment how much she loved him no matter what.

Marta attended Mass with Dominic and the others then joined them for lunch at the center. She and the boys cleaned up from their meal, forbidding Dominic from leaving his seat at the table, then went with them to the top floor to the gym. The players tossed the ball back and forth across the court as the onlookers cheered and Marta took pictures. Dominic yelled out instructions that Marta didn't understand, but she was thrilled by the fast-paced game and the hustling of the players. She couldn't imagine how many pictures she'd already taken.

When the game ended, Dominic jumped up and began slapping the boys on the back, congratulating the winners and giving pointers to the losers. Marta snapped photos of him and of his "boys" as he always referred to them. Disciples was more like it, she thought, and smiled at the way they all looked at Dominic. He was their mentor, their teacher, and their savior. He would balk at the notion of such things, but she had witnessed it first-hand over the past few days.

Since Dominic's trip to the ER, Marta had stayed close by his side and had the privilege of getting to know many of the young men at the center. Some of them were already acknowledging her as Dominic's girlfriend though neither she nor Dominic had placed any label on their relationship, nor had they moved past the getting to know each other again stage. They held hands and shared intimate details about their past and present, but Dominic, for all the love he professed, was holding back, and Marta knew that he worried about what the future held for them—if there was to be a future.

Marta felt a vibration in the pocket of her capris, and she pulled out her phone to see who was calling her. Anxiety crept in as she answered the call.

"Ciao."

"Ciao Nonna! Mi manchi. Quando tornerai a casa?"

"Isa! Mia cara," Marta said, filled with joy at the sound of her granddaughter's voice. She went out into the hallway and answered Isa in Italian, "I miss you, too. I'll be home in a couple weeks. Where is your papà? It's almost your bedtime, isn't it?"

"Papà and Mamma are downstairs. I wanted to talk to you, but they always call you when I am sleeping."

Marta smiled and shook her head. "Isa, do they know you called me?"

"No, Nonna. I called you all by myself. I'm big enough now."

Marta paced in the hallway outside the gym as she talked to Isa. "I'm sure you are, my love, but I think your papà would want to know that you are talking to me."

Ignoring this suggestion, little Isa went on. "Guess what I got today. I got a bicycle! Papà taught me to ride it in the driveway. I'm not allowed to ride near the road, but I can ride all around the vineyard when I'm good enough not to run into the vines."

Marta was taken back to her own youth, running and playing in the fields but always mindful not to go too close to the vines. Nicola had been raised in Fiesole, with roads and alleys, surrounded by other children. Life on the vineyard could be lonely for a child, sheltering even.

She thought of Dominic and his childhood in the city. What had it been like? She realized how little she still knew about the man to whom she had given so much thought throughout her adult life.

"Nonna, are you there?"

"Si, Isa, I'm here."

"Isa! To whom are you talking?" She heard Nicola's booming voice and Isa's small, repentant answer. "Nonna. I miss her."

"Isa, you know you are not allowed to make phone calls. Tell Nonna goodnight, and hand me the phone."

"Nonna, Papà says I have to say goodnight. I love you. Please come home soon."

"Lo farò," soon, she promised. "Ti amo anch'io." Marta listened as Nicola scooted Isa off to bed and called to Alexandra for help.

"Mamma, how are you?" he said when he finally got on the phone.

"I'm well, mio caro ragazzo. How are you and Alexandra and Carlos?"

"We are well. I hope Isa did not call you at a bad time."

"No, it is fine. I was..." What should she say? She had yet to tell Nicola about Dominic. "I was enjoying a basketball game at a local school."

"Basketball? You have never watched basketball. How did this come about?"

"I have become reacquainted with an old friend who enjoys the game."

"Ah," Nicola responded quietly. "So, you did find him."

Marta was speechless. "Mi scusi? What did you say?"

"Alexandra suspected that you were there to find someone, a man she was sure, someone from your past."

"Oh? What made her think that?"

"Mamma, you yourself have said many times how much you and Alexandra are alike and that you are like one soul in two bodies. So, is my wife correct? Is this friend a man?"

"He's an old friend, he and his brother. They lived near Zia Isabella when I was here long ago. I spent a lot of time with them and their cousin, Angela. Sadly, I learned that she has passed."

"Mi dispiace, Mamma." He paused before asking, "This friend, was he someone special? Alexandra believes he was."

Marta heaved a sigh. How intuitive of Alexandra. Had she known all this time, since their earliest conversation about Marta's summer in Baltimore, that there had been someone special? "Sometimes I think the bond between Alexandra and myself is too strong."

"That does not answer my question. Or perhaps it does," Nicola said.

The door to the gym opened, and the men filed out, followed by Dominic. He raised his brow in question, and she smiled. "Si, Nicola, he is someone special." Dominic went to her and slid his arm around her, and she nuzzled her head into the hollow of his neck. "His name is Dominic, and I knew him before your father and I married." She did not see the need to tell her son that she fell in love with Dominic while she and Piero were engaged.

The line was silent for a moment, and she thought for a second that she had lost him, but she heard his steady breathing and a swallow and knew he was contemplating his words.

"You will come home, will you not?"

"Oh, Nicola, of course I will come home. I miss you all terribly. Dominic is…" She looked at the man she knew she loved with all her heart and gave him a sad smile. "He and I are getting to know one another again, but I will return to you." As she said the words, she knew they were true, but she felt as though she was making the promise to them both, a promise that could only be kept for one of them. It was familiar ground, and she wished things could be different this time.

"Allora," he said with a sigh of relief. "We miss you, Mamma. Please be safe."

Marta promised she would, told him she loved him, and said goodbye, knowing that she was past being safe. She was in danger of falling completely in love with the second man who would precede her in death, and there was no net to catch her as she fell.

"So, you knew each other way back then and haven't spoken to or seen each other all these years?" Millie asked over the dinner she had cooked for them.

"It's true," Dominic answered. "We haven't seen or spoken since we were twenty-two years old, but," he said, looking at Marta, "she has been in my heart and in my thoughts every minute of every day since we said goodbye."

Marta felt herself blush but couldn't help but smile. The way he looked at her made her feel bubbly inside, like she would erupt with emotion at any moment.

"It all makes sense now," Millie said. "I always wondered why Dominic never married. He's such a catch." She winked at Dominic and he shook his head, laughing. Millie raised her glass. "A toast, to second chances."

Marta saw Dominic's smile falter, and the bubbles popped within her. Silence engulfed the room until Sally cleared his throat. "What my wife means is, a toast to finding each other again." He didn't have to add, *before it was too late.* They all knew that's what he meant, and

Marta felt sorry for Millie when her face flushed, and her eyes became filled with sadness.

"Of course, that's what I meant," she said, trying to smile.

"No," corrected Dominic. "You had it right the first time." He held up his glass. "To second chances. I let Marta go once, but this time, I'm going to hold onto her for the rest of my life."

Marta's eyes filled with tears, but she continued to smile as she held up her glass. She drained the glass of Belle Uve Amarone and let the familiar taste and warmth of it give her some comfort. Paul's restaurant had connected with Nicola's American distributor and now served all Belle Uve's products, and Dominic had picked up a bottle for tonight's dinner.

"So, tell me about your family's vineyard," Millie said, clearly trying to change the subject to a happier one.

Marta told them about the vineyard. She regaled them with stories about her childhood and how Nicola, who grew up hours away from his grandparents, must have been born with wine in his blood, for he had known since he was a little boy that he would one day take over the vineyard. She talked about her grandchildren, little Isa, named for her great-aunt, and Carlos, named for his uncle who died when Alexandra was in college. She boasted of her son's accomplishments and the many awards his wine had garnered, and all sad thoughts were pushed from the room as they talked and drank and laughed at each other's stories.

When the night was over, Dominic drove Marta back to her little house. As she unbuckled her seatbelt, he turned to her and said, "Are you sure you want to be there tomorrow?"

"Of course, I am sure. I will drive you to hospital and back and will stay with you while you rest."

"It's not going to be pretty, you know. I'm going to be sick and weak and—"

"Dominic, stop. You are not going to talk me out of it. Be here at nine o'clock, and I will be ready."

Dominic sighed in resignation. "I'll be here."

Marta leaned over and kissed him on the cheek. "And I will be here for you."

She held his gaze with her eyes and felt the heat building inside of her as his eyes changed from blue to grey, clouded by the heat building inside of him.

When he said her name, his soft, raspy voice sounded just the same as it had all those years ago on the dock under the stars. "Marta."

Just as it had then, his hand went to the back of her neck and tangled itself in her hair. He pulled her mouth to his, and she welcomed the kiss just as she had then. Though encumbered by the steering wheel and the console between them, they managed to wrap their arms around each other and lose themselves in the kiss.

Just as before, it was Dominic who broke away first. His breathing was rapid when he spoke.

"When you left, you took my heart with you. I never thought I would heal, but I did. In time, I found that I could love again, but I never loved another woman like

I loved you. Like I love you still. I know the pain and the heartache of being left behind. I don't want you to go through that."

"Oh, Dominic, do you think that I did not suffer the same pain and heartache? I needed to go home, but I didn't want to leave you. I have always carried my love for you in my heart. Just because I loved another does not mean that I did not love you."

"I don't want to leave you, to be separated again, especially since this time, it will be forever. I know it's sacrilegious to say, but I would give up Heaven to stay here with you."

"Don't say that," Marta admonished him sternly. "You are getting treatments. You have a chance. You can fight."

"But it will only prolong—"

"Who's to say that I won't die next month?"

Dominic looked stricken. "No!"

She took his hands in hers and held them tightly. "We have what God gives us. We will not waste it by counting days. Let's get through tomorrow and the next day and the next, and then we will see what we can do to make the most of the time we both have left. Nothing is promised to us. Another day is never guaranteed, but we must take each day we are given as a gift and thank God for it. We will find a way to share that lifetime we talked about. I will not listen to you talk of death or of leaving each other. We've loved each other for almost forty years, but we've shared little more than two months together. What time we share from here until the end, whenever that might be, will be time we are grateful for. Do not squander it by worrying about what will happen next."

Dominic closed his eyes and slowly nodded his head. He inhaled deeply and then looked at her, his blue eyes filled with love.

"You are the gift, my love. You are my life. I won't waste another minute thinking of my life without you or yours without me."

Dominic nodded but said nothing. He held her hand tightly as he walked her to the house and placed a soft kiss on her lips. After they said goodnight, Marta stood in the doorway and watched him walk back to his car and pull away. Then she sagged against the doorjamb and allowed herself to cry.

28 July 1983

It has been over a week since I have left the house except to go to Mass. I have said no to each of Paul's visits and resisted finding out what Dominic is doing. Each time they asked, I told Zia Isabella and Zio Roberto that I am staying close to spend my last few days with them. Today, Zia Isabella came to my room with her arms folded and a severe look on her face.

She said, "You have been moping around here for days. I know you miss home, and we will miss you when you leave, but there is something else going on. Tell me why you are hiding in this house? Did you and Angela have a row about something?"

Oh, how I wanted to tell her. I wanted to tell somebody. Angela is my only confidant. I can't even share with sweet Paul what I am feeling because I do not wish to stomp on his feelings. I needed to talk to somebody, somebody other than Angela, who is also sneaking around, but when I opened my mouth to speak, only sobs came forth.

Zia Isabella rushed to the bed and sat beside me. She put her arms around me and stroked my back, and it made me feel even worse. All summer, I have been lying to her, going behind her back, seeing the man she despises. How can I get her to see that he is a good man? And if I tell the truth, how can I regain her trust?

I wrestled with these things until I could not stand it anymore. I could not look her in the eye when I confessed. "I have fallen in love with someone who is not Piero."

Zia Isabella went still and was very quiet. "It is not Paul. He is still a child."

I shook my head and looked down at my hands fidgeting in my lap. "It is not Paul."

"Do I know this man?"

I nodded without looking up and without saying his name. I heard her long intake of breath, and then she released me and stood.

"I have done my best for you this summer," she said as she headed toward the door. "We have tried to give you a good experience and take you places. We have made sure you attended Mass and met the right people. What you have done, what I believe has been going on, is an insult to me and to our family. You must pack your bags. I will call Pablo and tell him that you are going home early. You cannot stay here any longer."

My sobs resumed as she shut the door. I wanted to scream. I wanted to beat my hands upon the closed door and call out that she was not being fair. I wanted to hate her, but I could not.

I have done this. I went behind her back. I betrayed her trust. I betrayed my family and Piero. And now I will go home and spend my life trying to make up for it.

Marta helped Dominic get back into bed after another trip to the bathroom. She wasn't sure she would have the strength to help him walk to and from his bed—the day she'd walked him to his car had been an act of sheer adrenaline—but she found that the old adage was true. Where there's a will, there's a way.

"Are you comfortable?" she asked once he was settled.

He forced a smile and reached for the glass of ginger ale on his nightstand that Marta had brought up to him. It was the only thing he thought he could keep down, but even that wasn't settling in his stomach as he'd hoped. "As comfortable as I can be."

She handed the glass to him and waited for him to take a sip then put it back for him. "Can I get you anything?"

"Maybe another blanket from the closet if you don't mind." He gestured toward the closet next to the bathroom, and she opened it, wondering how he could possibly be cold. The closet was neatly arranged with hanging clothes organized by type, racks of polished shoes underneath, and an array of linens on the top shelf. She reached for a blanket and shook it out, laying it over the one he already had.

"Your closet is much neater than I thought it would be. Years of bachelorhood?"

"Years of Mrs. Matthews cleaning the house, doing the laundry, and leaving me dinner at night. She's a lifesaver."

Marta laughed. "Allora, that explains how your house is as neat as a pin."

"It's certainly not my doing." He paused. "Hey, Marta, you know, you don't have to stick around. I'll be fine if you need to go."

"And where would I need to go?" she asked, hands on her hips.

"Anywhere but here. You're supposed to be on vacation. This is no picnic on the beach."

"We've never done that," Marta said. "Isn't the ocean close by?"

Dominic gave a small chuckle. "If you consider almost three hours close."

"That's not far. We should plan a trip there."

Dominic gave her a withering look. "Marta, I really don't think I'm in any condition to go to the beach."

"Not today." She clicked her tongue and frowned as she began to pace back and forth, her thoughts running wild. "In a week or two, you'll be up to it. No, we need to wait. Too many people. I did my research. I learned that you need to start being more careful about being around other people. Even a common cold could be a major setback to your recovery. No more dining out at fancy restaurants or visiting museums." She crossed her arms in front of her chest. "Why didn't you tell me that you should be avoiding crowds and staying close to home?"

Dominic shrugged. "I didn't know how long you would be here or how much time we would have. I didn't want to waste a minute."

"Uh-huh." She shook her head but kept moving. "Same old Dominic, following your heart instead of your brain." She regretted her words instantly and stopped walking, remembering the biggest mistake of his youth, but he just smiled.

"If only I had followed my heart all those years ago, but we said no regrets, so I will let it go. When do you propose we make this trip to the beach?"

She began pacing again. "How about the fall when there aren't as many people around. I want to be able to stroll in the sand, barefoot, hand-in-hand, with the sun beating down on us. I'll buy a big floppy hat for me and a paglietta for you. Even in fall, we have to protect our skin."

"A what?"

Marta stood still and looked at Dominic. "Hmm?"

"You're going to get yourself a hat and me a...what?"

"A paglietta." She tightened her lips in thought. "A hat. Like a gondolier."

Dominic managed a hearty laugh. "It sounds like a pastry I could get at Vaccaro's."

She ignored his comment. "I will have Nicola send me one, an authentic one. You will be the most handsome man on the beach."

"Are you trying to hide my baldness?"

She sent him a shocked expression. "I love your baldness. I told you it makes you look like James Bond."

"When Connery played Bond, he had hair," he said wryly.

Marta looked at her watch. "You need to rest. It's been a long day."

"Changing the subject, are you? Not really into bald men after all?"

Marta drew the curtains in front of the window. "I'll be in the soggiorno if you need me." She bent down to kiss him on the cheek, and he caught her arm, his reflexes still quick.

"I think it's sexy when you talk in Italian."

"And I think you are... what is the word for it? When the medicine makes you pazzo?" She twirled her finger by her head. "It did the same for Nicola after he fell from the roof a few years back."

"Do you mean loopy?"

"Si, you are loopy. Have a nap. You will feel better when you awake."

"Only if you're still here," he said, beginning to sound drowsy now that he was comfortable and the room was darkened.

"I promised you I would be." Then she recalled what she had said to Nicola many times as a child after they read Tolkien's *The Lord of the Rings* together. She repeated the beautiful words of the Elfin Queen Galadriel, "Do not let your heart be troubled. Tonight you shall sleep in peace. Sweet Dreams, Dominic."

"Of you..." he whispered.

"Special delivery," Paul said when Marta opened the door a couple hours later. She leaned in and kissed him on both cheeks. "Rigatoni with marinara for you, and spaghetti with olive oil for Dom."

"Thank you, but shouldn't you be working?"

"I've got other chefs who can cover. Besides, it's a Monday. I never work on Mondays."

"Si, I forgot. Allora, it's been a long day. It feels like Monday should be over."

Paul dropped the bags onto the kitchen table and turned to look at her. "You look tired. I told you I could do this. You didn't have to spend the day taking him to the hospital and then looking after him."

"And I told you that I wanted to."

"For how long, Marta?" Paul's face tightened, his eyes narrowing and his lips pressing together.

"I don't know what you mean," Marta answered, turning to take the carry-out cartons from the bags, the scent of marinara and garlic pushing the smells of body fluids and sickness from the house.

"You do." He reached for her arm and made her stop fooling with the cartons. "Marta, look at me."

She turned but could not look into his eyes, the eyes of the boy who knew her so well.

"Marta," he said quietly. "You have a life, a family, and a job on the other side of the world. This could go on for weeks, if we're lucky he might have a few years. How long until you break his heart again and go back home?"

Marta gasped loudly and pulled her arm away. She bored her eyes into his. "How dare you? I would never break his heart."

"Yet you did. And it took him years to get over it, but he never got over you. I saw how you two were the other night, and I saw the way he looks at you. That hasn't changed. He spent thirty-six years waiting for you to come back, and now you're here, like Florence Nightingale, trying to nurse him back to health. It's not going to happen, Marta. I've been to the doctor with him. I've read all the pamphlets and the websites, and the books for grieving families. Have you? Do you know what he's up against?"

"I have," she spat back. "I searched online. I read about the treatments, about the medicine they will have him take, about his chances."

"It's all good and well that you read about his physical condition, but what about his emotional condition? Forget about the cancer. What about his heart?"

Marta felt the tears, hot and wet as they brimmed from her eyes. "What about my heart?" She raised her voice, unable to control her own emotions. "I loved him. I would have stayed, would have broken my engagement for him."

"But you didn't."

"I couldn't!" She shouted. "I wasn't given a choice. As soon as Zia Isabella found out about us, she sent me home. What would you have had me do? Run away, make Dominic take me somewhere, have him get into more trouble? I didn't leave because I didn't love him. I left because I did."

It was the first time she had said the words out loud, admitted them to anyone, including herself. She felt her knees buckle and grabbed for the counter to steady herself. Paul reached for her, and she felt his body stiffen. She looked up and saw that his eyes were wide and his face pale. She followed his gaze and felt her breath catch in her throat. White-faced, with his hands gripping the doorjamb, stood Dominic.

"What do you mean, Zia Isa made you leave? You wanted to stay?"

Marta looked from Dominic to Paul and back to Dominic again. "I desperately wanted to stay. I told her that I was in love with you. She called my father, and they made arrangements for me to fly home the next night."

"And that morning you came to say goodbye."

She nodded, her tears flowing uncontrollably.

"Why didn't you tell me?"

"I couldn't. I loved you, but you were not in a good place. I knew that. If I had told you, what would you have done?"

"I would have found a way to make it work!" Even through his nausea and pain, he had the strength to yell, and she knew his anger fueled him to fight. "Dammit, Marta. We could have been together. We could have—"

"What? Run away? Skipped your parole? Caused you to be brought up on kidnapping charges?"

"We were adults."

"And you were on parole! I knew what that meant. I didn't when you first told me, but..." She looked at Paul.

"I explained it. After you told Marta how you got into trouble, I explained what it meant to meet with your parole officer every month, that you had to check in or you'd be sent back to juvie, or possibly to prison."

"I couldn't be the reason you were sent away again. I knew you were a good man with a good soul. I knew God had a plan for you. And I knew that I had to leave, to marry Piero, and to try to forget about you. But I never did. I never forgot. And I'm here now." Her voice had grown shrill and even she heard the desperation in it. "Please. Please understand. I have loved you since the first day I saw you. I left for you, so that you could rebuild your life without the scorn and resentment of my family."

Dominic's eyes were clouded with pain, or perhaps grief. She didn't know which, but she knew that she had hurt him and that he needed time to process what he had just learned. She reached for her purse on a nearby chair.

"I will go. I am sorry. When you are ready, you know how to find me." She locked eyes with his. "I'm not leaving this time. I'll be back when you want to talk."

Before they could stop her, Marta turned her back on both men and walked out the door. She walked to the corner and hailed a taxi. She called Antonella and woke her up, crying nonstop throughout her retelling of the day, letting her friend try to console her but not feeling any better. By the time she got to the house, she was exhausted from the day's activities as well as from grief. She went straight upstairs and collapsed on the bed, not too tired to cry like a child until she fell sleep.

Chapter Ten

29 July 1983

Clouds surround the plane as it makes its way toward Italy. It seems that everyone on the plane is asleep but me. Zia Isabella made me promise not to tell anyone back home about Dominic. She said that Papà will tell only Mamma. She said that I will be ruined if Piero refuses to marry me, but will I? Won't that give me a reason to return to Baltimore, to return to Dominic?

But it's no use. We are through. Zia Isabella drove me to the automobile shop this morning and waited in the car while I told him goodbye. She did not want to, but I begged, and she allowed me this one time to see him that was not in secret, one last time to be able to tell him goodbye.

The look on Dominic's face when I slowly walked into the automobile shop was one of pleasant surprise until he read my own expression, then his face tightened the way it does when he is worried. How well I've come to know his expressions and read his moods in such a short time. It's as if I have known him my entire life. And I realized at that moment that I have. He is so like my father.

Papà almost died in the War. He was thought dead for a very long time. He was wounded physically, mentally, emotionally, and even spiritually. I am told that he shut down for a very long time, that he was angry with the world, and that for a while, he did not want to live. He did not tell me this. It was Zia Isabella who shared it with me many years ago when we came to visit her, and she marveled at how happy my father was.

Even now, he sometimes closes into himself, when memories are too much for him to bear. His expressions read like a children's coloring book, black and white illustrations that tell a story without words.

As I stood and looked at Dominic, I saw so much of my father in him, and I knew that I was right to tell him goodbye. He is still wounded and needs time to heal. Maybe he was right. Maybe I helped him begin that process, but he needs to find his own way, to fight his own demons, and to discover what God has planned for him. He cannot do this if we are in a battle for our love. Sometimes, love comes at a cost, and I knew in that moment that Dominic does not yet have what it will take to pay the price.

"What is it? What's happened?" He asked, rushing over and taking my hands, transferring black grease onto my palms and fingers. I paid no mind. "I tried to get word to you, to see you. I've been so worried. Paul said you wouldn't leave your room. What's going on?"

"We need to speak," I said. "Is there somewhere we can be alone?"

Dominic searched my eyes and then called to another man that he would return soon. He led me to a room in the back and closed the door behind us. He looked down at his hands and then at mine and took me to a sink in the back of the room where he rubbed a gritty ointment onto my hands that smelled faintly of oranges. I closed my eyes and tried to memorize the way it felt as his hands caressed the cleaner into mine and gently rubbed out the grease. The feel of the gritty cleanser, the warm water, and his soft touch combined to produce a somewhat sensual effect, and I began to waiver but steadied myself for the necessary task. There was no choice. After Dominic rinsed my hands, he handed me a clean towel, and I dried them before turning to him. His eyes held mine.

"Please, tell me what's wrong?"

"I am leaving. Tonight. I am returning to Italy."

The pain on his face was almost unbearable, but I did not look away. I needed to steel myself, to harden my heart against what I knew he would say.

"No, don't go. Please, stay, We can make it work. We can run away if we have to." It was as though he had read my thoughts. I knew his words before they tumbled from his mouth, this man who was but a stranger a few weeks ago now speaks to me without words, his heart to mine.

"We can't," I said quietly. "I must go. You see..." I swallowed the obstruction in my throat. "I am to marry when I return. I cannot stay with you."

Dominic reeled back as though he had been shot. His eyes widened, and he clutched his chest. "Married? But you... we... I don't understand."

Oh, how it pains me even now when I recall and write his words, the look on his face, the pain in his eyes.

I closed my eyes and bit back my tears. "I have been engaged to Piero for two years. He is working for my father now but will begin teaching at university in September. He has bought us a house. It is all set."

Dominic shook his head in disbelief. "No," he cried. "It can't be. You love me. I know you do."

I looked away from him. I could not stand to see him in pain. The room smelled like the barn on the vineyard—oil and cleaners and other heavy scents I could not identify filled the air in the closed-space around us, and it made me feel dizzy. Or was that feeling caused by what I knew I had to say? I had to tell him the truth, even if it was only half true.

"I love Piero," I said out loud while my heart shouted so loudly I thought he might hear it, 'and I also love you.'

When I looked back at Dominic, the pain had been replaced by anger. He squeezed his hands until they turned white, and he spoke through gritted teeth.

"So, I was nothing more than the American you wasted your summer with. A summer fling. Well, you had your fun. Now, go home and marry your Piero, or whatever his name is. It's not like I care." He turned and placed his hand on the doorknob, and I cried out.

"Dominic, no. It's not like that. Please."

He turned to me, and the look on his face left me stricken with grief. "Go home, Marta. Have a nice life."

I began crying. "Please, don't," I called, but he was gone.

Zia Isabella and I returned to the house. When I placed my foot on the bottom stair, she put her hand on my arm and stopped me. I turned to her, and she looked at me with pity.

"Mi dispiace, cara. Someday, you will understand. This is for the best."

The sky outside my window has turned dark, and the light above gives me little light with which to see, so I will end here. I will not write in this journal again. It is filled with moments of joy that I will keep in my heart forever, but it is filled with too much sadness and heartache. I will marry Piero, and I will love him the way a wife should. I will pledge my vows, and I will do everything I can to forget about Dominic and all that he means to me.

Marta opened her suitcase and reached into the zippered pocket on the inner left-hand side. She carefully removed the small leather book that she'd kept hidden away since that night in 1983. She gently slid her hand across the smooth cover, and her fingers trembled as she opened to the first page. On the plane back to Italy, she had calculated that exactly eight weeks, fifty-six days, and eighty-thousand-six-hundred-and-forty minutes took place between the first entry and the last, but looking back now, it seemed like the time was in some ways shorter and in other ways longer than that period of weeks.

Her fingers brushed the ink, the handwriting of long ago almost strange to her now. She had not written so many words in English before then nor since. Reading the first page now, the words felt foreign to her, as though it was someone else's story being told, but the feelings were the same. She turned a few pages until her eyes fell on the first mention of his name. Her finger caressed the word as if she was caressing the back of his hand. So much time had passed. So many things had happened. They were older, wiser, more experienced. This time around should have been different. The feelings should have melted away, and they should have been able to reminisce and laugh and then walk away, knowing that they had grown into different people who thought of each other fondly but had no ties that bound them together.

Allora, that isn't what happened. The years apart only seemed to tie them more tightly to each other, twisting and turning the knots until the only way they could breathe was through a common breath. Their hearts had melted into one, and all that they felt back then had intensified with time and age. Their years apart had molded and shaped them into a new creation, as a potter molded and shaped a fine pot, sturdy and resistant to breakage. Or so she had thought until she saw the look on his face when he heard the truth.

She had intended to tell him when the time was right. She was certain that the knowledge that she had loved him and had wanted to stay with him would only increase his love for her. She was so sure that he would understand why she obeyed her aunt and her papà and had gone home, had married Piero, and had made a life without him. Now she knew that he saw it as something different—as a betrayal of their love, of her taking the easy way out, and as a sign that she did not have the will or the desire to fight for him.

As she looked at the writing on the pages, scrawled by her hand, she wondered if he was right. Perhaps she had chosen the easier path and had done so selfishly. While she told herself that she was protecting him, was she really protecting herself? After all, what is eight weeks? Was she afraid that, if she stayed, his love for her would wear off, that they would realize that they were not meant to be? And where would that have left her? Would her family have welcomed her back? Would Piero? She knew that one of those answers was yes, but the other? They had loved each other, yes, but had Piero known about Dominic, would he have told her to leave? The truth was, she did not know, and throughout the many years of their marriage, she was unwilling to find out.

It was late morning by the time she finished reading her words, the words of love and loss. She had not heard from Dominic or Paul, and she wondered if she had lost them both. Should she pack her bags and go home? Was it right that history repeat itself, or had God brought her here for another chance? If so, what should she do?

St. Dominic, Mother Mary, St. Leo the Great, somebody, please hear my prayer. Help me to know what to do. Please send me a sign.

She was about to put the journal back when a folded piece of paper fell to the floor. She bent and picked it up, recognizing the letter she had written without any intention of sending it. She slowly unfolded the yellowed paper, careful not to let it rip at the folds, pressed into place for thirty-six years. Tears ran down her cheeks as she read the words, even more unsure than she had been back then about whether she should have sent it. Certainly, this was not the sign she sought. Not knowing the answer, she carefully placed the letter in her pocket, unsure as to why she did so, and put the journal back in her suitcase.

She went downstairs to find something to eat, realizing she hadn't had anything in almost twenty-four hours. As she descended the stairs, she could feel the pangs of hunger as well as the lightness in her head.

As she neared the bottom step, she saw a movement outside the window that framed the front door. Before she could process who might be there, the doorbell rang.

She didn't peer out the window but took a deep breath before opening the door. Paul stood on the front step, and her heart lurched at the sight of him. He had dark circles under his eyes, and his face was empty of all color. Her hand went to her chest as though she couldn't breathe.

No, her thoughts screamed. *I have cursed myself by asking for a sign rather than trusting God.*

She held her breath and swallowed before speaking. "Dominic?" she asked with apprehension.

"He had a rough night," Paul said. "It was much worse than the first time. I'm not sure if he'll make it through all of the treatments. They take so much out of him."

He was okay, alive at least. She breathed a sigh of relief and reached for Paul's arm, saying a silent prayer of thanksgiving.

"Come in, please."

He followed her into the house, and the heat of the summer day that came in with him was swallowed up by the cool air that circulated inside the house when she closed the door.

"I was going to make a panini. Would you like one?"

"Sure, thanks," Paul said, following her then taking a seat and looking around the little kitchen. "This place looks exactly the same."

"Si, Alexandra and Nicola thought about updating it when they considered selling it, but in the end, Alexandra decided they should keep it the same. It was Zia Isabella's favorite room of the house, and so much of her is still here, like a phantom hovering over us."

She thought about that for a moment. It was Zia Isabella who had made her leave, and her phantom's presence should seem like a haunting to Marta, but instead, it felt like the soft, cool breeze of a spring morning, welcoming and comforting. Perhaps Isabella, from her heavenly perch, knew that the time was finally right. Was that the sign she needed, the feeling of her aunt's loving presence during this time of uncertainty? If so, what did the sign mean?

"She never told us, you know, that she made you leave. Not even when we became close to her."

"Zia Isabella was good at keeping secrets," Marta said. "She kept many over the course of her lifetime."

She thought of teenaged Isa's journal, the one Alexandra had discovered hidden in the barn that revealed Isa's secret fondness for Roberto, her silent suffering when he was at war and when he returned a severely wounded man, her clandestine work with the Resistance, and her cover-up of the events that led her and Roberto to flee their homeland.

"Is it true?" he asked. "Is it true that you loved him and didn't want to leave?"

The knife in her hand hovered over the tomato for a moment before she turned and looked at Paul and nodded. "Si. I couldn't say it out loud, even to myself until the moment I admitted to Zia Isabella that I had fallen in love with him. Until then, I was telling myself that I could resist him, that I loved Piero and that it would be my choice to leave Dominic and return home. Once I said the words out loud, I knew I could not leave. But then it was not within my control. Without the blessing of my family, I could not stay. It would have been no good for him, for either of us."

"He sees that now. We talked most of the night as he wasn't able to sleep between the sickness and the aches and pains he suffers. He wanted to come himself, but he's still too weak and too dizzy when he stands. He didn't want to call. He asked if I would come."

Marta smiled as the sandwiches sizzled on the stove behind her. "Just like old times," she said.

"I was thinking the same thing." Paul stood and went to stand next to her as the scents of fresh basil and melting mozzarella rose from the pan. "Sophia is the only person who still cooks for me, now that Nonna and Mom are gone. Thank you." Marta nodded and smiled at him. "I still need to know. What are you going to do? Are you going to stay or go this time?"

Marta bit her lips together and kept her gaze on the paninis. She inhaled and exhaled slowly before looking at Paul. "Honestly? I do not know. I need to talk to my son, to explain, to let him know that…"

"That you still loved his father no matter what may have happened in the past."

She nodded and flipped the sandwiches over. "Nicola is a very understanding man. He will be all right, but I need to talk to him about what I should do. I have a job, a house, responsibilities back in Firenze—I can take a leave of absence after my vacation ends, that is worked out—but there are other things I do for my city and my church, and there is my family of course." She turned to Paul. "I do not want to leave him again, but I do not know how to do this, how to make this decision, how to pause my life and—"

"Marta." Paul laid his arm across her shoulders. "Dominic will understand if you don't stay. He'll be okay. I'll make sure he's okay."

But would she be okay if she left him again? For the first time since she left Italy, Marta knew what she had to do, and she felt it with all the conviction of her heart. "No, I want to stay. I will stay. This time, nobody is going to send me away."

Marta knocked on the bedroom door. It was dark but for a faint light peeking between the window curtains.

"Come in," Dominic said. "I'm awake."

She went to his bedside but hesitated. Should she sit at his side or in the cushioned chair that Paul must have dragged into the room? Not sure, she stood and gazed down at him.

"I am sorry for yesterday. I did not mean to wake you with my outburst nor to upset you."

He reached for her and pulled her onto the bed so that she sat facing him. "I'm sorry. Sometimes I forget that we were barely more than children at the time. I can't imagine what you were feeling, how torn you must have been, and to have to face your family after the way we hid things from them. It must have been very difficult for you."

"And for you. I wanted to tell you that I loved you. I wanted you to know that I didn't want to leave, but as you said, we were so young, and there was so much uncertainty."

"There is still uncertainty," he said quietly.

Marta shook her head. "No, there is only love." She pulled the letter from her pocket. "Do you mind if I turn on the lamp?"

Dominic shook his head, but his eyes held a wariness. "What is that?"

She switched on the lamp, and the soft glow was almost blinding, but her eyes quickly adjusted. She held up the yellowed letter, realizing just how old and worn it looked, barely intact at the folds. She stared at the letter, recalling that last day, those last minutes before she left the house. She had to tell him the truth. She could not leave him the way she had, with all that pain and anger. She knew she had to explain, so she wrote it down; but in the end, she knew she could not send it.

"It's a letter I wrote to you after that last time we saw each other. I wanted to explain, to tell you how I felt, but I was afraid—"

"Of me?" His pain was audible, and she was quick to shake her head.

"Of us, of the feelings I had for you, of what might happen if you knew the truth. I didn't want to hurt you, and I knew that if you knew the truth, it would hurt you in the long run."

"Because of my past."

She pressed her lips together and nodded.

"Read it to me, please. I want to hear it. Even if it can't change what happened, I want to know what you would have told me if you could have."

With trembling hands, she unfolded the letter and began to read.

29 July 1983

My dearest Dominic,

Words cannot express the dagger to my heart knowing the pain I have caused you. I pray that you will read this meager letter and will understand why I have left, and why I said the things I did.

You are right. I do love you. I love you with all my soul even though I know that to be a sin. In a short time, you have become the sun and the moon to me, and I long to be with you. But this cannot be.

Zia Isabella told me that someday, I will understand why I had to tell you goodbye. I acted like I would never understand, but that is a lie. You see, I do. I know that what we have, while it is worth all of the lies and secrets we had to create, would be a hardship on us both.

I have come to know you and to love you, and I know that you are good and kind and loving, but my family does not see this, and if we were to go against their wishes, that would not change. You would always be a scourge to them and, in their eyes, to me. If we were to go away together, that would create more trouble for you, and where would that leave us? I am but a girl in a strange land, and you are but a boy with a need to redeem himself.

I never intended to fall in love with you. I have loved Piero for so long. I am sorry if that hurts, but I say it only to show you that this, what we have, came as a surprise to me. I tried to stop myself, to tell myself that whatever I was feeling was not real, but I could not resist the pull you have on my mind, my body, and my heart. I long to be with you no matter what my conscience tells me, no matter what is right in the eyes of my family or in the eyes of God.

The night we kissed, I knew that there was no going back. You had taken possession of me, wholly and completely. I was petrified to see you again. I stayed away, locked in my room, a prison of my own making. When Zia Isabella asked what was wrong, I thought I could finally tell her, that she would see how much I love you and that all would be well.

Instead, she reminded me that we were playing a game with broken rules. I do not want to leave you. I did not want to tell you goodbye today, and it pains me to recall the hurt in your eyes, but I know that Zia Isabella is right. I must return to my life in Italy, and you must find a way to make a life for yourself here.

You are good, Dominic. You are worthy. You will be a great man someday, and I will count the days, even if they number the stars, until I can once again look into your eyes.

I will be forever yours.

Marta

She folded the letter and slipped it back into the envelope before wiping away the tears with the back of her hand. The room was silent as she refolded the envelope. She went to put it back in her pocket, but he reached out and stopped her.

"May I have it? Please? After all, it was meant to be mine."

Marta nodded and laid it on the nightstand.

"I had forgotten about it until earlier today when I found it in my journal from that summer. I needed to push those thoughts away. Once my plane landed in Italy, I was Piero's betrothed once again, and I had to return to my proper role in life." She looked at Dominic. "It was no easy task. I thought about you day and night. I begged Zia Isabella for news, but she would not oblige. I was so worried about you, but Angela, dear sweet Angela, she let me know that you were just fine. She told me of all the women you went out with, none of them from the neighborhood, and how you were doing just fine."

"She lied," he said quietly. "I told her to tell you those things. Part of me wanted you to be jealous. Another part didn't want you to know that I spent most of my days at the shop and all of my nights locked in my room thinking of you, missing you, and looking at the one photograph I had of us."

"The one at the pool?"

"No, my photograph. Nobody has ever seen it except for Paul." He gestured toward the drawer of the nightstand, and she opened it.

Beneath a small Bible was a faded picture of the two of them. They were looking at each other and laughing, and she recognized the harbor behind them. "Who took this?" she asked, feeling bewildered.

"Paul did. Do you remember how you inspired him to take up photography? He bought that camera. Remember? The one he had at the pool. He took it with him almost everywhere for the longest time. He gave me that picture the day before you left. I almost ripped it up, but I couldn't do it."

She nodded as the memories came back to her—teaching Paul how to focus, how to line up a shot, how to frame it just so.

"He did a very good job. It is…perfect."

"That's just how I always thought of it. It perfectly depicts that summer, the time we spent together, how happy we were, how much in love."

The photo left no doubt. As they laughed, they gazed into each other's eyes with unmistakable love and trust. The way their bodies melded together made it seem as if they were one, Siamese twins with shared hearts.

"I don't have photos of us and only one of you. I was so afraid to take them, so worried about our secrets being exposed."

"That's the only printed photo I have of you. Paul has a few that are in Mom's albums, but I have many other pictures of you that I have carried in my heart."

She looked at him and smiled. "And I of you."

He smiled back warily. "I'm so tired today. I don't think I can get out of bed. Can you, will you stay with me?"

She changed positions so that she was lying next to him. "There is no other place I would rather be."

When Marta returned home that evening, having allowed Sally to take the night shift, she felt as if everything had changed. Zia Isa's phantom still hovered over the kitchen, and Marta smiled as she let her aunt's presence flow over her, realizing now that the ghost was not there to send her away again but to welcome her back.

"You were right. I knew it then though I didn't want to. I was meant to marry Piero, to have Nicola, to adopt Alexandra as my own as you did and be blessed with their little ones. That is the life that God planned for me. But he put me on this other path as well. Dominic and I needed to meet each other. We needed to fall in love, to experience pain and heartache, to lose and to find each other again. God gave us each the lives we were meant to live, but he also brought us together. I need Dominic now as much as he needs me, and though you tore us apart, you also brought us back together."

She looked around the room at the faded yellow walls and the deteriorating cookbooks standing on the counter. She ran her fingers along the island where Zia Isabella rolled out many cookies and kneaded breads and other pastries and cut strips of pasta, where Marta sat and talked and read letters from home, and where she and Angela drank lemonade and gobbled cookies.

"Alexandra believes with her whole heart that you left her a share in the vineyard so that she and Nicola could meet. I believe that is true, but there was more to your plan, wasn't there? You also left her this house, the very house that I lived in, the house where Paul came to the door to fetch me and where Angela and I snacked and listened to the radio. This is the house where I dreamed about a life with Dominic and where you told me those dreams could not be. This is the house just down the street from Dominic's family home, and you knew that someday I would return. By leaving this house to Alexandra and inserting her into our lives, you guaranteed that Dominic and I would meet again. You knew that he was waiting for my return."

Marta snorted a quiet laugh. "For someone who did everything she could to keep us apart, you are quite the matchmaker."

From nowhere, a slight breeze wafted past Marta, and she suddenly smelled the fragrance of roses, the same fragrance that her aunt had always worn. She closed her eyes as warm tears rushed into them. She inhaled the scent and savored it before it disappeared as quickly as it came.

"Alexandra always says that your ghost is still with us, and I believe it is true. I let myself hate you for a very long time, but now it's time to put the past in the past where it belongs. Good night, Zia Isabella, and thank you for the many gifts you have given us. I love you."

She took one last look around the kitchen before switching off the light and heading to bed. After a follow-up text to Antonella, she slept as she never had before with no heartache, no pain, no weariness, and no apprehension. She fell asleep recalling the words she whispered to Nicola so many times, the same words she whispered to Dominic the afternoon prior. *Do not let your heart be troubled. Tonight you shall sleep in peace.*

It did not matter how much time she and Dominic had spent together in the past nor how much time they would have in their future. Zia Isabella's immortal magic, and the hand of God, had brought them together then and now. That was all that mattered.

Chapter Eleven

"Are you nervous?" Dominic asked as she set up the laptop on the table in front of them.

"Should I be?"

"This is a big deal. Even if it's through the lens of a camera, it's a big step."

"I always find life easier to deal with through the lens of a camera," Marta said truthfully. She tapped a series of buttons, and the mechanical music played. She watched in anticipation as the screen changed and the images emerged. They were all four gathered on the sofa in front of the large picture window. The curtains fluttered behind them, and Marta recalled the many nights Alexandra and Nicola sat right there huddled over Isa's journal. Marta was there for some of those nights, and they were all amazed at the life Zia Isabella had lived before she was even eighteen. Allora, the trials of youth, Marta thought, during times of both war and peace.

"Ciao, Mamma!" Nicola said in Italian. "It is wonderful to see your face!"

Her heart leaped at seeing his smile. She answered in English so that Dominic could understand. "Nicola, how I have missed you! And Alexandra, you are glowing. How are you feeling?"

Her daughter-in-law's blush shone across the miles. "Grazie, Mamma. I feel well. This one has been much easier on me than either of the other two."

"Meravigliosa. I am so happy to hear that." She waved at the screen. "Isa e Carlos, i miei amori, you are getting so big!"

"I am almost six, Nonna." Isa held up three fingers on each hand. Her English was very good, thanks to her mother, and Marta was suddenly even more grateful that Zia Isabella had sent Alexandra into their lives.

"Si, you are growing older every day." She turned toward Dominic and took his hand in hers and squeezed it. "I have somebody I would like you all to meet." She inhaled deeply. "This is Dominic, he and I met here in Baltimore thirty-six years ago."

Isa scrunched her nose and tilted her head. "Were you babies?"

Everyone laughed, and Marta nodded. "In some ways, cara, we were."

Dominic cleared his throat. "It's nice to finally meet you all. I've heard a lot about you."

Nicola smiled. "I have to admit that, until a week ago, I had heard nothing about you, but Mamma has filled me in on quite a lot in the last few days."

Leading up to this moment, Marta had called Nicola every night that week, easing him into the knowledge that Dominic was more than just a 'special friend.' She assured him that their first time together was one of deep friendship but that this time, it had blossomed into more. It was what she and Dominic had agreed upon. There was no use in causing Nicola to question his parents' love for each other.

"Why don't you have any hair?" Isa asked, as precocious as always.

Dominic laughed. "I shaved it off. It's very hot here, and I thought this would be easier to take care of. Don't you have bald men in Italy?"

Again, her nose scrunched, and her head tilted as she shook it from side to side. "I don't think so."

"Isa!" Alexandra scolded. "You know that's not true. Father Rulli is bald."

"But he's not *that* bald, Mamma."

"I'm afraid this is true," Nicola said with a laugh. "He does have hair on the sides of his head."

Dominic laughed, too. "I'm hoping mine will grow back," he said. "In time." He looked at Marta, and she saw the hope in his eyes for more than just hair.

"I remember you," Alexandra slowly said, a look of recognition dawning on her face. "You used to visit Signora. And your brother, Paul, right?"

"Yes, that was me. And Paul. I remember you, too, Alex. You were the light of Signora's life that last year she was with us."

"Why didn't you ever mention Marta?"

Dominic shook his head. "What would it have meant to you at the time? I had no idea you would end up knowing each other, and Isa and I had an understanding. We didn't talk about the past. It was, ah, painful for us both."

"What do you do, Dominic?" Nicola asked. "For a living, I mean."

"My best friend and I run a center, a shelter of sorts, for young men who have gotten into trouble or have nowhere to go. It's my life's work and my passion. The boys and young men are like family to me."

Alexandra gasped. "Signora used to give money to the center, a hefty sum, each month. I always wondered why that cause mattered so much to her, but when I asked, she answered, something to the effect of, 'I was once wrong about someone, and this allows me to make amends for doubting him.' I never knew what she meant, and I had no idea you had anything to do with the center."

Marta felt Dominic's grip tighten. "What? Isa gave money to the center?" He looked at Marta, his eyes wide and mouth open in shock. "Not long after she passed, we received a large amount of money from an anonymous donor. The letter stipulated that the money be used to create a scholarship for any young men wishing to pursue an education in art or photography." He slapped himself on the side of the head. "How did I not see? How did I not recognize that it was from her and that it was meant as…" He looked at Marta. "As what? A peace offering? To make amends? Or as a reminder?"

Marta shook her head. "I am stunned. I did not know she had left anything to anyone other than Alexandra, but it makes sense. She and Zio Roberto never spent a dime. They had to have had a huge savings. With no children and a modest home in a low-cost neighborhood, they must have put away quite a lot of money."

Nicola coughed, reminding them that they were not technically alone. "What was she trying to make amends for? What was the reminder of?"

Marta and Dominic shared a look, an unspoken agreement, and Marta nodded at him.

"Alex," Dominic began, "when you knew me, Isa and I were on good terms, but that was not always the case. When I was young, a teenager to be exact, I made mistakes. I was involved in some wrongdoing, so to speak. Marta and I met the summer she was here and began spending time together along with my brother, Paul, our cousin, Angela, and her boyfriend. But Isa did not approve of our…friendship." He looked at Marta, and again, she nodded.

"I still do not understand what she had to make up for," Nicola said.

Marta heaved a deep sigh, not sure she was ready for this. She had not planned on telling Nicola the whole truth, but the conversation had taken an unexpected turn with the revelation of Zia Isabella's support of the center. Marta closed her eyes and tried to arrange her thoughts into words.

"It was Zia Isabella who made me return home to Italy to marry your father." As soon as she said the words, she knew she had said them wrong, made them sound like something they were not, or perhaps it was the truth finally coming to light.

Nicola was quiet, and Marta saw the myriad of emotions cross his face. He opened his mouth to speak but closed it, blinking several times, then shaking his head and looking away as though facing her would be too much. "Mamma, you did not want to come home and marry Papà?" She heard the hurt in his voice and said a quick prayer that the Holy Spirit would guide her in her explanation.

"No, Nicola. It was not like that. I loved your father very much. It was just…"

"Just as when Nicola was expected to marry Eva but discovered he was in love with me," Alexandra said quietly, laying her hand upon her husband's knee. "You had a very big decision to make, but I suspect it was much harder for you. You loved them both."

Marta nodded, tightening her lips. "Very much. I did not want to choose or to hurt anyone. I think Zia Isabella knew that, so she chose for me." It might even have been the truth, now that she knew all that she did about her aunt and her matchmaking prowess.

"And you stayed with Piero all those years, devoted to him and to your family. You left Dominic and made a point not to look back or allow what might have been to ruin what was." Alexandra said this to Marta, but she was looking at Nicola. "How hard that must have been."

"No, not once I was home. Like you said, I made my decision. I loved Piero. I married him, and we had Nicola. We were very happy for a very long time. I would not change that if I could. You must know this."

Nicola finally moved his eyes back to the camera. "You loved Papà. I know this. I saw it every day until he died and even after. You were devoted to him, to us."

"Sì, I never stopped loving your father, not ever."

"But you never stopped loving Dominic either." His voice was quiet but resigned, no longer sad and not accusing.

"I tried to," she said quietly. "I didn't allow myself to think about him, not ever, not until…" She looked at Alexandra. "A few years ago, when you first came, I told you that I spent the summer here. It was then—"

"Why did you wait so long after that?" Alexandra asked.

"Piero was still alive, you remember? His heart attack was a few weeks later. When you reminded me of that summer, it was a pleasant memory, but that was all. I had lived with just that memory for so long, and I never dreamed I would ever come back, that we would ever meet again."

"But it's been five years," Alexandra pushed, and Marta was reminded what a spitfire her daughter-in-law was.

"I needed to be sure that Nicola would be all right, and I needed to know that I would be strong enough to accept whatever I found here. I had not seen or talked to or heard from Dominic in all those years. I did not know what or if or…" She looked at Dominic for help, but Nicola spoke up.

"You did not know if the love was still there."

"Si, I did not know. When I was asked to come to Washington for work, I felt that it was a message from God. It was finally time to find out if there was anything there, if there ever had been or still was."

Nicola looked at Dominic. "And you are still in love with mi mamma?"

Dominic looked at Marta and smiled before turning back to the camera. "I am. Very much. In fact, I have never loved another."

Nicola looked at his wife and their children. His uncharacteristically stoic expression gave way to a smile, and he turned back to his mother and Dominic. "Then I would like to bring the children and Alexandra to America to meet you, perhaps after the harvest. They have been without a grandfather since birth. It would be nice for them to meet you." His voice broke as he spoke the last sentence, and Marta felt her eyes filling with tears.

They would still need to tell Nicola about Dominic's illness, and Marta still needed to decide what to do about her job and her house in Florence, but it was decided. She would stay with Dominic as long as he needed her, and he would, somehow, become a part of her family like he always should have been.

Marta was awakened to the humming of her phone. The morning light that haloed around the shades in her bedroom told her that it was later than she normally awoke. She hadn't slept well over the course of the past week, with the worry over Dominic and the anxiety about how Nicola would take the news of their relationship, and she supposed the lack of sleep had finally caught up with her and plunged her into a deep, restful slumber. She groggily reached for the phone before awareness tumbled in and a bad feeling crept up her spine causing her to throw off the covers and grab the device from the nightstand. At the sight of Paul's name on the screen, she stifled a cry and pressed the button to connect.

"Paul? What is it?"

"You need to come right away. To the hospital." She heard talking in the background, and Paul answered in a muffled tone. "Marta, I've got to go. Hurry." Without any explanation, he was gone.

Marta saw that it was well past nine already. She leapt from the bed, grabbed a pair of flowy white pants from the closet, and threw on a pale pink blouse. Her toothbrush barely touched her teeth before she tossed it onto the counter and raced down the stairs. She wasn't out the door before she stopped. Which hospital? Which floor? The ER? Oncology? Paul had been in such a rush, and obviously was distracted, and he didn't tell her anything she needed to know.

She leaned against the wall, her purse in hand, trying to figure out what to do. She called Paul back, but he didn't answer. She pressed the selection for his home phone, but there was no answer there either.

What time is it now? What day? Where is Sophia? Where is her daughter, Antonia? Why is nobody answering?

She stared at her phone as if it had all the answers, but it only told her the day and time. She would have to figure out the rest.

Marta took several deep gulps of air and tried to focus. Once her breathing was under control, and she could begin to have some semblance of rational thought, she dialed the center. It was the only number she had other than Paul's.

"Seton Center," a voice said. "May I help you?"

"Tony? Is this Tony?"

"I'm sorry. Tony had a family emergency. May I help you?"

"It's me. I mean, it's Marta. Dom's Marta. Do you know what hospital they're at? Paul didn't tell me. He just said—"

"Hold on, Miss Marta. Take a deep breath, and slow down. It's Reggie. I don't know what happened, just that Tony got a call to go to the hospital. Are you trying to get there, too?"

"Si, I mean, yes. Please, can you help me?"

"Yeah, they're at Mercy. Do you need a ride? I can send someone to pick you up."

Mercy? Where is that? Is it the hospital? That's not where I took Dom before.

Her thoughts raced through her mind, and she recalled that Mercy was where Dominic had his chemo treatments. She had driven him there in his car, but she had no car of her own. She found her calm and took a breath before answering. "Si, can someone help me, please? Do you know? Is Dominic all right?"

"I'm sorry, Miss Marta. Like I said, I don't know anything. I just know that Tony came in a little while ago and then got a call from his dad to head to Mercy. I don't know what's going on. He didn't say it was Dom. I mean, he would've told me, right?" Reggie's voice faltered, and Marta worried that perhaps she should not have called, should not have upset anyone at the center.

"I don't know. I don't know what is happening."

"Okay, stay calm. Give me your address. I'll call Sally."

Marta rattled off the address, her mind swirling with questions and trying to come up with answers. Not Hopkins, which was good, right? No mention of Dominic by Tony. She thanked Reggie and disconnected the call. Not knowing what else to do, she sank down onto the front step and waited.

What felt like hours later, Sally's Fiat pulled up in front of the house. Marta's feet never touched the ground as she flew to the passenger side and opened the door. She threw herself inside and slammed the door.

"What's happened? Is it Dominic? What's going on?"

Sally shook his head. "Dom says he's fine. He says he just took a fall, but that he's going to be okay."

"What do you mean, 'he just took a fall?' Where? When?"

"His housekeeper found him this morning on the bathroom floor. She called an ambulance and then called Paul. Dom fell and hit his head. He's going to be okay, I promise you."

"And he's at Mercy?"

"Yeah, that's where his doctor is. The lung cancer specialist is at Hopkins, but Dom wanted to go to Mercy, so that's where they took him. It sounds like everything is going to be just fine."

Though his words were reassuring, his frantic driving said otherwise. He took the corners too fast and sped up at yellow lights. She braced herself on the dashboard as a car slammed on its brakes and honked its horn at them. It was like being in a taxi in Rome.

"Sally, slow down. If Dominic is okay, why are you driving like a crazy person?"

Sally let out a breath and cursed. He came to an easy stop at the next light and turned to Marta. "You're right. I'm sorry. Paul says that Dom swears he's okay. He hadn't seen a doctor yet when I talked to Paul. When Paul called, I thought..." He shook his head. "Well, you know what I thought."

She did, and she understood his panic, but as worried as she was, she wanted to get to the hospital alive and well and not in an ambulance of her own.

When they pulled into the parking lot, she saw Tony and his twin, Antonia, standing outside the entrance. They both ran to her and Sally as they approached the building.

"He's okay," Tony said. "He's really okay. Everyone panicked, but the doctor said there's nothing to worry about. He's awake and talking and yelling at us all to go home."

Marta and Sally exchanged looks. "Well, that sounds like Dom," Sally said.

"Why did he fall?" Marta asked.

"He says he got dizzy and tried to grab the side of the sink but missed and fell. He's got a great, big shiner and a dent in the side of his head, but he's cussing up a storm and telling everyone to calm down and stop fussing over him."

"That makes me feel even better," Sally said as he made his way through the automatic double doors with the rest of them on his heels. He raced past the greeters at the desk, and Marta heard Tony rattle off their names and the room number.

"Third door down, Uncle Sal," Tony called, and Marta hurried to keep up with Sally, grateful when he was stopped by security guard and had to wait for Tony to hand them their visitor stickers.

Tony led them to Dominic's room, but Marta could have found it on her own based on nothing but the loud voice booming across the ER.

"I'm telling you all, I'm fine. There's nothing to see here. Go home."

Marta went into the room, and Dominic's eyes grew so wide, she wondered what he saw when he looked at her. She reached up to her hair, not sure that she brushed it, and realized she hadn't put on a hint of makeup. Did she really look that bad?

"They called you, too? For the love of Pete, I'm fine."

She rushed to his side and peered closely at his black eye. "Si, you look just fine."

"You look like your house caught on fire. Calm down. It was just a fall."

Typical of any Italian household, the room was buzzing with the sound of voices. Paul was filling Sally in on what they knew. Sophia was on the phone to somebody, giving assurances that Dominic was all right. Tony and Antonia squabbled over who was going to sit in the lone chair. Before Marta could say another word to Dominic, two more people bustled in, and she recognized Paul's two oldest children.

"People, people!" A voice shouted from behind Marissa and Adrian. "This is the ER, not happy hour at Sabatino's. Now, either quiet down or clear out."

Marissa and Adrian moved aside, and a maybe-forty-something, nice-looking man walked in wearing a white coat with a stethoscope tucked into his pocket. He looked at Paul.

"Pauly, get your brood out of here so I can examine my patient. I don't know how you all managed to be allowed in here at once." He turned to Sally. "You, too, Sal. Come on, give me some room." They parted ways like the Red Sea, but Marta remained by Dominic's side. There was no place for her to go.

"I'm sorry, ma'am. I need to get there."

"Of course," she said, looking around for some place to stand.

Paul spoke up. "Alrighty, fam, time to get outta here. We've got a restaurant to run, and Uncle Dom's in good hands." He shooed and waved, and the room cleared as though he was a magician casting a spell with his gestures.

"I'll be right outside," Marta told Dominic, and she and Sally made their exit.

"The doctor?" she asked. "Someone else from the old neighborhood?"

"You catch on quick. What was it that gave him away? The Italian-American accent or the name, Palumbo, on his coat?"

"The way he talked to you and Paul. Pauly?"

Sally laughed. "Not many people call him that. We're all in the Knights together down at the church."

"Of course, you are. And I suppose he volunteers at the center in his spare time?"

"Nah, he just writes big checks a couple times a year. To be honest, he was one of ours."

Marta looked back toward the room. "The doctor? He was one of the boys who used the center?"

Sally nodded. "He didn't just use it; he lived there for about three years. Spent most of high school there before getting a scholarship to Mount St. Mary's in Emmitsburg to study medical biology and then moving on to the University of Maryland Medical School. You know Father Leo?" She nodded though she only knew the name and what Dom had told her. "He was at the Mount Seminary for a while, used his connections to get the kid in. Just another testament to the miracles Dom has worked through the years."

"You know, I keep hearing that America is so very different from Italy, but the longer I'm here, the more I see that they're very much the same. Everyone seems to be connected somehow."

"It all depends upon where you are, I guess. Baltimore is a smaller city than it seems." Sally looked down at his watch. "Hey, listen, I'm due in court in an hour. Can you manage to get back home? If you and Dom need a ride, you can call my office. Someone will come get you."

"We'll be fine. Thank you for bringing me. I'll let you know if there's any more information to be had."

Sally thanked her and said his goodbyes just as Dr. Palumbo walked out from Dominic's room.

"He can go home in a little while. I've talked to Dr. Hunter. The dizziness is normal, but it might be worse for the next few days. I'm going to keep him for just a little while to make sure we haven't missed anything, then he can leave. He had a nasty fall. I'm not going to do a CAT or anything. His vitals are good, and he's had enough radiation pumped through him already. If anything changes or worsens once he's home, give Dr. Hunter a call. Dom says you'll stay with him today. Marta, right?"

"Si, I am Marta. Thank you. May I go in?"

"Sure, sure. If nothing changes, a nurse will be in later to get him to sign his release papers. It was nice meeting you. See you all at church on Sunday."

He waved and walked away, and she detected the click somewhere in her brain. Of course she knew he was from the neighborhood. She'd seen him at church with an army of children. She wondered how many other men she'd run across at church or at a restaurant or even at the market whose life had been touched and perhaps altered by Dominic's hand.

She went back into the room and was surprised to find it so quiet. She walked to his bed and leaned down and gave him a soft kiss.

"Dr. Palumbo says you're probably well enough to go home, but he's keeping you for just a while longer to make sure."

"I'm well enough to leave now. It was just a fall. Nothing major."

"Have you looked in a mirror yet?"

He frowned and waved a hand in dismissal. "Do you know how many black eyes I've had in my lifetime?"

She was certain she didn't want to know the answer. "Are you sure you're feeling all right?" she asked as she perched on the bed next to him. The rail had been lowered, but it was still awkward to find a comfortable way to sit.

"I feel fine. A little headache is all." He reached for her hand. "Hey, I'm really sorry. We're supposed to be making the most of our time together, and we seem to be spending all of it in hospital rooms."

"As long as we're together, I'll spend time with you anywhere." She leaned in to give him another kiss, and he pulled her to him. She'd lost track of how long they'd been kissing when she heard someone clearing their throat from the doorway. Marta blushed as she turned to look at the nurse, but the nurse just smiled.

"I'm just checking on Mr. D'Angelo. He'll be out of here soon. I just need to check his vitals for now."

Marta stood and let the nurse do her job. When it was finally time for Dominic to be released, Marta stayed back and listened carefully to the discharge instructions and wondered if this was how their relationship was going to be from here forward.

She shook away the thought. She meant what she had said to Dominic. As long as they were together, she didn't care where they spent their time.

"Tell me something I don't know about you," Dominic asked, closing his book and putting it on the end table beside him.

It had been a few days since Dominic's trip to the ER, and they were at Dominic's house, having a lazy afternoon, the kind that was often required by the heat and humidity of a Mid-Atlantic summer day. A lamp with a dim bulb was the only light turned on, yet the room shone bright with the afternoon sun. A fan swirled overhead, its rhythmic drone, Marta noticed, tantalizing both of them to close their eyes and be lulled to sleep. The faint scent of coffee and sausage with eggs still lingered from their late morning breakfast.

Dominic sat on the tweed, navy blue couch that matched the armchair nearby, his legs stretched out and feet propped on a pillow on the dark brown coffee table. Marta was curled up on the other end of the couch, leaning against a pillow, assessing the photos she had taken over the past couple weeks. She closed her laptop and set it aside, then stretched, arching her back, lamenting the aches and pains of getting older.

"Something you don't know about me? Allora, that could take a while."

"I know. I've been thinking about it, and as much as we've talked since you've been back, I still feel like there's so much I want to learn."

"Like what?" He had her curious, and she wondered what he wanted to know that she hadn't already thought to tell him. The rest seemed so unimportant now.

"Oh, I don't know. Tell me about Piero."

Marta blinked. "Piero? That's not something about me."

"But it is," Dominic said, looking intently at her. "You loved him. You left me to marry him." Before she could protest, he held up his hand. "I'm not trying to put you on the spot about that. He was a part of your life for a long time. I want to know about this man who is a complete mystery to me, your husband, Nicola's father."

Marta took a long, deep breath and thought about where to start. "We met at university. Though he was older and was a graduate student, we had a class together and joined a study group. After a while, the group became a duo. We started doing everything together, and eventually, we realized we'd become a couple."

"No first date or electrical shocks or fireworks or any of that kind of stuff?"

"It wasn't like that," she pushed back. "I knew that I loved him for a long time. The relationship itself just happened...slowly." *Much differently than what happened between us. I knew instantly that I was drawn to you. I knew the feelings I had for Piero weren't the same, but...*

"Marta?"

She abandoned her thoughts and reminded herself that she was talking about Piero. "He was a good man, conscientious, kind, intelligent. He was a very attentive husband and a, um, a well-intentioned father."

Dominic raised an eyebrow in question.

"He was a good father. He loved Nicola, and Nicola idolized him."

"But...?"

Marta sighed. "He was an academic. Books, learning, school, having a solid career that meant something, those were important to him."

"But not to Nicola."

"The only thing that was ever important to Nicola was Belle Uve. He saw it as a career that meant something, and he tailored his studies toward making it a success. He even came to America and got his master's, without arguing, at his father's insistence."

"But Piero wanted him to do something different?"

Marta made a noise through her nose. "Anything different. Piero just didn't see a future in wine-making."

"But Nicola has done very well for himself."

"He has, and his father was very proud of him for his hard work, but he thought Nicola was throwing his education and his finances down the drain, as you say. He never had a chance to see just how successful the vineyard became. He passed away just after Alexandra showed up, and it wasn't until after she arrived and introduced new ways of doing things that Nicola really began selling enough wine and making enough of a name to make a nice profit. Now, his wine is heralded all over Italy."

"Interesting," Dominic said.

"What is?"

"I know that Alex knew nothing about wine or running a business. I believe she was, like you, more into the arts. She used to play piano a lot and take pictures."

"Si, she and I are a lot alike. And she may not know much about business, but she knows a good deal about design and how to get people to pay attention. She's very smart and very good at coming up with ideas. I think she just needed someone or something to inspire her."

"And that was Nicola."

"I think it was the whole package. I think it was the knowledge that Zia Isabella had confidence in her, that she knew Alexandra could help the business, that Alexandra was given a fresh start, and that Nicola desperately needed help even though he was too stubborn to admit it. They challenged each other in ways both good and bad, but it was just what they needed. *They* were just what they needed."

Dominic sat up with his elbows on his knees. "Did Piero give you what you needed in life?"

She could tell by his tone and expression that he was asking the question in all sincerity.

"He did. He tried very hard to be a loving husband, to have a stable and happy marriage, and to be a good provider. He worked hard at his profession and at home. We were a good fit."

"I'm glad," Dominic said, settling back onto the couch. "I always prayed that you had married a good man who would take care of you."

Marta looked away to hide her pained expression.

"What is it?"

She couldn't look at him when she answered. "I wish I could say the same." She looked down at her hands, twisting them in her lap. "I was happy, and I wanted you to be happy, but a part of me never wanted you to look at another woman the way you looked at me."

She raised her eyes slightly to gauge his expression. A slow smile spread across his face, and after a moment, he began to laugh. His laughter grew until he started coughing and had to reach for his glass of water on the end table. He downed the entire glass before he looked back at her. She had no idea what he found so funny.

"What was that about?"

"I always knew there was a spitfire hiding under that guise of innocence. I feel better knowing that you have at least one flaw."

"Ha! Just wait. The longer we're together, the more my flaws will begin jumping out at you."

"The more the merrier. You'll have to have a lot of them to catch up with me."

"Oh yeah? And then what will you think of me?"

He moved faster than she thought he could with the medications, the chemo, and all that he was battling. In a flash, he was hovering over her, his arms bracing himself up in the couch.

"I'll think that you got your wish. I have never and will never look at anyone the way I look at you. You are all I've ever wanted. I love you."

Her heart pulsed as she looked up at him, and she looped her arms around his neck and pulled him down onto her. "I love you, Dominic. With every breath I take. Flaws and all."

Chapter Twelve

Two days later, the same din from the hospital room could be heard in Terre e Mare despite the fact that the restaurant was closed and doors were locked. Pockets of conversations were spread around the room, and the mixture of laughter, wine, and Italian spices created an intoxicating atmosphere.

Marta felt Dominic saddle up behind her and put his arms around her waist. He nuzzled his cheek against hers. "Are you glad we came?"

"I am, but I'm still worried about you being around this many people. You're supposed to be staying away from crowds."

"This isn't a crowd; it's our family. Besides, I couldn't take another whole day and night at home."

Marta looked around the room, gazing from face to face, each of them bearing the most remarkable resemblances to each other. Brothers, sisters, cousins, nieces, and nephews all gathered in the main dining room of the restaurant to celebrate Paul's fifty-third birthday. Marta was beyond thrilled to be here for this family celebration. She only wished Paul's cousin, Angela, was there with them. She smiled at William and Angela's grandchildren sitting at a table and coloring with Paul's grandson. As she watched them, she realized what Dominic had just said.

"Did you just say, 'our' family?"

"I did. And not to steal my baby brother's thunder, but I think we should make it official."

Marta turned to look at Dominic. "Mi dispiace. Can you say that again? I'm not sure I understood."

"You understood me all right. Let's do it. Let's get married. You and me."

"Quiet, everyone," Tony yelled. "Mamma's bringing out the cake." As Sophia appeared in the doorway with a cake that must have had every fire department in the city on alert, Tony led them all in singing *Happy Birthday*.

Marta joined in, grateful for the interruption. When the singing stopped, Dominic leaned down and whispered in her ear, "Don't think you're off the hook. I'm going to keep asking until you say yes."

Marta held her breath as she watched Paul blow out all fifty-three candles. Dominic's proposal, such that it was, was what she had been waiting thirty-six years for. She should have shouted a resounding yes and flung her arms around him while squealing with delight. Instead, she said a silent prayer that what they were doing, pretending that everything was normal and that all would end well, wasn't just a game of Russian Roulette.

Marta stood in the doorway of the gym, looking at the man on the bottom bleacher. Only two months prior, she had stood gazing at this same man, a man who looked almost exactly like he had when she knew him so many years ago. Allora, had she arrived in America today and come to the center to seek him out, she would not have recognized him.

In addition to the baldness, he had lost so much weight that it looked like he was wearing hand-me-down clothes from a sibling twice his size. His eyes were hollow, and his skin was as pale as the gym walls. He sat apart from the others in the room, obeying doctor's orders about protecting himself from germs, but no matter how hard she and Sally tried, they could not keep him from his boys. Nearly a week of sitting at home day and night was more than he could stand.

As though she controlled him like a marionette, his gaze turned toward her, and he smiled. She smiled back and went to sit next to him.

"Who's winning?" she asked.

He took her hand in his. "I am."

Her stomach turned in that familiar way it did whenever he said something that truly touched her heart, and she leaned into him. He wrapped his arm around her, and they stayed that way until the end of the game. This time, Dominic did not get up, did not give high fives or slaps on the back. The players air pumped as they walked by him and several thanked him for coming by to watch. When the last ball had been bounced across the floor and the room grew silent, Marta sat up and turned toward Dominic.

"Yes," she said, and he tilted his head and frowned.

"I didn't ask you anything."

"But you did. A few days ago, at Paul's birthday party."

His eyes widened, and his mouth broke into a wide, happy smile. "Do you mean it?"

She nodded. After three days of prayer and deep introspection, along with many texts and phone calls with Antonella, she had decided that marrying Dominic was precisely what she was meant to do. God brought them together and gifted them with this great love that had lasted through two different lifetimes—hers and his—through years of being apart but hearts always connected. Who was she to go against God's will?

Not since the day she had told him goodbye had Marta seen tears in Dominic's eyes, but there they were, glistening and brimming over, threatening to flow down his cheeks. "I've waited my entire life to hear you say that one little word."

"I think it's about time to finish what we started that summer so long ago."

"Was it really that long ago?" he asked, his voice choked and the tears coming full force now. "It feels like I saw you for the first time yesterday, standing on the sidewalk in shorts and a t-shirt, your hair tied back behind your head, with a camera hanging around your neck. You were so beautiful, you took my breath away." He looked her up and down. "You're still as beautiful today."

"I think the treatments have affected your eyesight. I hardly resemble that girl."

He cupped her chin. "You've never looked more beautiful to me."

His kiss sent waves of longing from her lips to her toes and every intimate place in between. She felt her mind go blank as all thought was washed away by his cleansing touch, a baptism of love that symbolized the beginning of their new life together.

The image appeared on the screen, and Marta felt simultaneous waves of excitement and trepidation. How would Nicola take the news?

"Ciao, Mamma! It is good to see you. We all miss you so."

"I miss you, too, cara. I truly do. Where is everyone?"

"The children are in bed, and Alexandra is giving us time alone. Your text sounded important, and she thought, perhaps, private."

Marta's heart began to beat wildly. *Can I really do this? Can I tell my son my plans, our plans? Are we really going through with this after all this time, all these years?*

"Mamma, is everything okay?" Nicola leaned toward the screen, his eyes widening in worry.

"Nicola, there are some things I have not shared with you."

His eyes narrowed, and she saw a familiar look, one of suspicion and wariness. "Mamma, what is going on? Does this have to do with Dominic?"

"Si, there are some things…" She faltered. She had yet to say the words out loud, and they pained her. To say them would make it too real, more than the chemo or the loss of hair or the dizzy spells. To say them transformed them from a possibility to an inevitability, and she was not ready to accept it. She took a deep inhale and spoke before she could stop herself again. "Dominic is not well."

She heard Nicola's sharp intake of breath, and he tried to hide his surprise, but he always had been so easy to read. Slowly, she saw understanding dawn on his features. "His hair. I should have wondered about it."

"Si, he has lost his beautiful hair. He is weak and dizzy some of the time, but he is doing remarkably well."

"It is cancer," Nicola said without question.

"Si, it is cancer. In both lungs."

"How long, how much, I mean…"

"Three weeks to three years. We do not know. After the chemotherapy, he will begin taking some experimental medication. We do not know how well it will work."

"There is more," Nicola said, able to read her as well as she could read him.

"Si, Dominic has asked me to marry him."

Nicola frowned. "Mamma, how can he ask this? You've only been there for two months. You hardly know him."

"I do know him, Nicola. I've always known him. He has always been a part of me, of my heart."

Nicola looked pained, and his features hardened. "This is not right. He is taking advantage of you. He will need much help in the coming months. You do not want to be condemned to be his—"

"Nicola, I would do it willingly just as I would have for your father, just as Alexandra did for you after the accident. I love him, and I left him once. It was the right thing to do then. I would never have had all those wonderful years with your father. I would never have had you. But this is the right thing to do now. He needs me, and for however long he can be in my life, I need him."

Her son was quiet, a look of deep contemplation shadowed his face. His brow was furrowed, and his mouth was set in a straight line. Finally he said, "You have made up your mind."

Marta nodded. "I did not answer him at once. I prayed and I thought long and hard. I did not want to accept out of pity or regret but out of love. I do love him, Nicola. I hope that does not pain you."

"No, Mamma, it does not. I can see that you love him, and I could tell on the last video call that he loves you very deeply. I would not want you to be alone. Papà would not have wanted that, but in the end, when Dominic is gone, you will be alone again."

"But I will have had what most never have. I will have had the chance to marry and be with both men I love with all my heart. I will have had the chance to celebrate two lifetimes instead of one."

Nicola nodded. "It will be difficult, perhaps more difficult than losing Papà. You had him for many years, but you will have Dominic for only a short time. And Papà went suddenly, but you will have to watch Dominic go. It will be very painful even if only for a brief time."

"And I will cherish every moment."

After a beat of silence, Nicola spoke. "I told you that we would like to go to America after the harvest. I think it is time now. We should meet your Dominic in person and be there for the wedding."

A wave of gratitude washed over her. "Oh, Nicola, I would be so happy, but what about the vineyard?"

Nicola's face contorted into concern for only a brief moment. "We will make things work. This is important."

A noise of surprise escaped her throat. "You have never thought anything was more important than the vineyard. Are you sure?"

"Si, si, do not worry. Carlos e Giovani e Maria will have things under control." Though he said the words, she saw the doubt in his eyes.

"If it is too much…"

"No, it is not. We will come. When, uh, when will you and Dominic…?"

"When will we be married? Not until you arrive, I promise. I do not want to do this without you."

Nicola smiled. "I am glad. There is one thing though; there is not much room in the house."

"You're right, but I have a better idea than everyone staying at the house. Leave it to me to make the plans."

"Si, Mamma. I will make arrangements and let you know when we can be there. We will try to hurry. Ti amo."

"And I love you, Nicola. Thank you, thank you."

Marta worried that the flurry of activity that took place over the next month would be too hard on Dominic, but even with another chemo treatment under his belt, he looked stronger and healthier than she had seen him all summer. She was looking down at the legal pad in her hand when he caught her around the waist and pulled her down onto his lap at his round, oak kitchen table.

"You need to slow down. You're spending too much time worrying. Everything is going to be perfect."

Marta sighed. "There is so much to do. The guest list and the cake and the flowers and the menu—"

"Paul has the menu under control. Sophia is baking the cake. Millie has already helped you with the flowers. The guests have all responded. Everything is being taken care of."

She looked at him and felt a rush of love mingled with a sense of apprehension. "Are you sure you are up to this? It is so much. We could just meet with Father Sebastian in a quiet ceremony and not have all of this fuss."

"Paul and Sophia would never speak to us again! You know how Italians love big celebrations."

"Si, and this is another thing I am afraid of. The size of the wedding is too much. You should not be around so many people or having such a big day. We must be care—"

His mouth met hers and ceased her talking and her anxiety. When he pulled away, his grin was wide and mischievous. "You talk too much. And you worry too much. It is only family who will be there, and I do not have to worry about too big a day because you will do all the worrying for me. Relax, Marta. Everything will be fine."

She smiled and closed her eyes, leaning her head against his cheek. "You are right. It will all be well."

"Be honest with me," he said, and she lifted her head to look into his eyes. "Are you this nervous because of the wedding or because your family will be here tomorrow? Are you worried about Nicola and how he will handle all of this?"

Marta started to shake her head no but stopped. "Maybe I am worried about what he will think and how he will feel. His mamma is going to marry another man. That cannot be easy."

"Then we'll make it easy for him."

"How will we do that?"

"By showing him how much we love each other."

Her heart melted and she relaxed into the familiar comfort of being cradled into him. A smile formed on her face as she thought of what was to come. Her son would be at her wedding. How special that would be. How could anything go wrong with all of her loved ones gathered together to celebrate such a precious day.

As soon as the thought crossed her mind, she wished she could take it back.

Marta was both nervous about Nicola's reaction and worried about Dominic's health as she waited by the curb behind the wheel of Paul's family car. Airplanes zoomed overhead, some coming and some going, as she watched the sliding doors with nerves that were saturated with as much electricity as the hot, humid air around her.

She watched person after person but did not see her family though they had texted her that they had arrived and were going to get their luggage. She peered through the windshield at the threatening sky. Thick, dark clouds clustered in ominous bunches, heavy with rain, reminiscent of the last of the ripe, heavy grapes threatening to fall from the vine. A loud crack of thunder shook the car, and she let out a small cry.

She turned back toward the doors just as a familiar little girl appeared, wearing a pink summer dress, her long dark tresses falling over her bare shoulders. Marta opened the door and stood, waving to them with all the exuberance of the uncorking of a new bottle of sparkling wine. She hurried around the car and found herself enveloped in an octopus hug, eight arms stretching and circling around her. She felt the hot tears on her cheeks as she was released and came up for air. She gently pinched Isa's cheeks and then Carlos's. She wrapped Alexandra in as big a hug as she could, noticing how round and ripe she had become since Marta had left Italy. She laid her hand for a moment on the swell of Alexandra's belly, smiling through her tears as she looked into her daughter-in-law's eyes. Finally, she turned to Nicola and placed her palms on each side of his face.

"Mia cara, Nicola. How I have missed you."

From behind her, Marta heard a voice say, "What about me? Did you not miss me?"

Marta turned, her mouth open and her mind filled with shock. Her best friend of thirty-five years stood on the sidewalk, suitcase in hand. Marta squealed like a child and ran to Antonella. The two women hugged, then air kissed, then hugged again.

"You did not tell me you were coming."

"I wanted to surprise you."

"You did! It's the best surprise ever."

She led Antonella to the car, and everyone began speaking at once as they loaded all the luggage into the trunk and settled in for their ride into the city.

"It's a good thing I borrowed Paul's car instead of driving Dominic's. With all the luggage, the car seats, and my wonderful surprise, we would never have had enough room to fit us all."

"Mamma, where is Dominic?" Nicola asked as though just realizing her mother's fiancé was missing. "Were you both not to meet us?"

Marta tried to prevent the frown from forming on her face and smiled bravely. "Dominic was not feeling up to coming this morning, but you shall meet him soon."

"Is he all right?" Nicola asked with a heavy dose of concern in his voice.

"Si, he has good days and bad. Hopefully tomorrow will be a good day." She turned and smiled at Nicola briefly before looking back at the road.

"Is this America?" Isa asked.

"Si, little one. It is the United States of America. There are many countries in America, North and South, and this is one of them."

"Are there bicycles in America? I wanted to bring mine, but Mamma said there is not room to ride it here." Marta heard the pouting in Isa's voice.

"There are many, many bicycles here, but our house is on a very small but busy street."

"I told you I had a bicycle, Isa, that I rode to your Prozia Isabella's house every day, even in the rain, but we could not bring yours on the plane."

"Is yours still here? Is it at the house?"

Nicola looked toward the backseat and smiled. "Si, Isa, Mamma's bike is in the basement, but it is too big for you. Maybe next time."

Marta wondered about the words 'next time' and thought about Dominic, home in bed with a fever that had suddenly appeared the previous afternoon. Would there be a next time for their family to be gathered here in Baltimore? One that was not shrouded in mourning?

She forced her morbid thoughts away. She was getting married tomorrow. Only happy thoughts would be allowed.

"Mamma? Did you hear me?"

"Mi dispiace, Nicola. Can you please repeat?"

"Mamma…" His voice was quiet, and his hand was firm when he placed it over hers on the steering wheel. "Are you all right?"

She smiled. "Si, mio figlio. I am fine. All will be well."

She said a silent prayer that her words would reach God's ears and be his will.

Marta was relieved to see that Dominic looked better when they arrived at the restaurant that evening. She had tried to convince him to cancel the rehearsal and the dinner, and though he did relent a bit—there would be no rehearsal at the church-- he refused to cancel dinner with their families. He assured her that he was fine, and that Dr. Palumbo had made a special house call just to be sure. She rushed to him and fell into his arms. "You are better?" she asked.

"I am now," he said, leaning down and kissing her deeply and meaningfully. "Now, where is our family I'm just meeting?"

Each time he referred to anyone as 'our family' it made her heart flip. She loved him so and was counting the minutes until they truly would be one big family.

She took his hand and led him across the room.

"Dominic, this is mio figlio, Nicola. And you remember his beautiful wife and my dear daughter, Alexandra."

Rather than extend his hand in greeting, Dominic leaned in and kissed both Nicola and Alexandra on each cheek, sending Marta's heart into more acrobatics.

"It's so good to meet you, Nicola, and to see you again, Alex."

Marta felt a tug on her skirt. "And me," Isa said.

"Allora, cara." She leaned down and gave Isa a kiss then straightened back up. "And this is little Isa and her brother, Carlos."

Dominic bent down and first kissed Isa on both cheeks and then Carlos. "I'm so happy to meet you both. I've heard a great deal about you."

"Papà says that you and Nonna will be married tomorrow and that I will carry flowers down the aisle at the church."

"Yes, Isa, that is correct. And Carlos will carry the rings."

"But the flowers are more important, right?" She batted her eyes at him as she asked her question as though the picture of innocence. Marta knew better.

"Isa, both jobs are important," she admonished her granddaughter before turning to Antonella. "And this is Antonella, my closest friend, and now, my maid of honor."

Dominic air kissed Antonella. "I've heard so much about you. Thank you for coming."

"Prego. It is my pleasure. I had to make sure Marta was choosing wisely." She looked him up and down and smiled. "I think she has chosen well."

"I'm glad to know I passed that test," Dominic said with a laugh.

Marta turned to Nicola and took hold of his arm. "Come, meet Paul and the rest of the family."

Dominic laid his hand on her arm to stop her. "In a moment," he said. "First, I have some business to take care of with Nicola."

Marta looked at Dominic with one raised brow. "Oh? And what is this business?"

"A time-honored tradition that I would not think of overlooking."

"I see people eating," Isa said with a note of impertinence in her voice. "When can we eat?"

Antonella took her hand. "Come, cara, Zia Antonella will find us something to eat. Carlos, you can come, too." She reached for his hand, and they headed toward a buffet table of appetizers.

Marta and Alexandra watched Dominic and Nicola as they stood in the only quiet corner of the restaurant.

"He is very handsome and very charming," Alexandra said with a smile. "I always liked him."

"He is," Marta agreed as she watched Nicola smile and nod his head, reaching out to shake Dominic's hand. Dominic took the hand and then pulled Nicola into a hug. She saw her son's surprised expression soften, and Nicola gave Dominic a hearty pat on the back as they released each other.

"I believe my husband just gave permission for his mother to be married," Alexandra said.

Marta felt her heart leap within her chest. "You have no idea what that means to me." She could hardly say the words, and she wiped away a tear as the men returned to them.

"Are you ready?" Nicola leaned down and whispered in her ear as the march began to play.

Marta stood in her ivory linen suit with a skirt that fell just below the knee. Unlike her first wedding, in which she wore a full-length white gown, there was no veil on her head, and her bouquet was a modest yellow rose nestled in a soft bed of baby's breath and fern.

Isa followed Antonella, dropping satin petals down the long aisle, and Carlos stood on the altar, clinging to the legs of his new cousin, Tony, whom he already adored after just one evening together. Marta could see Paul but could not see his brother beside him from her spot behind the door.

"Si." *I have been ready for a very long time.* She smiled up at her son, and his look made her wonder if he could read her thoughts. His smile was sincere, but his eyes were heavy with sadness. "Are you ready?"

Nicola nodded. "Si, I am ready to see you happy again, not alone. I just…" He shook his head. "Papà would be happy for you."

She felt her heart tug and squeezed the arm that held hers. "I loved him very much."

"I know, and he loved you." Nicola nodded his head toward the inside of the church. "And so does Dominic."

Marta closed her eyes and swallowed. She inhaled deeply and calmly said, "Let's not keep him waiting."

She never felt her feet sink into the plush carpet as Nicola led her down the petal-laden aisle. The packed church might have held all of their friends and family or total strangers, for she couldn't see any of them. The lights and candles might have lit up the church with the brightness and glory of Heaven, but it all seemed dark to her as her eyes only held the glow of Dominic's smile and the luminosity of his eyes. When Nicola placed her hands in Dominic's, she felt her breath leave her, and the rest of the world fell completely away.

The Monsignor—a title and honor she hadn't known about Father Sebastian until they began planning the wedding—welcomed everyone and began the Mass, but his words fell on Marta's deaf ears. She sang the responses and hymns without thinking of the words. She listened to the readings they had selected, but she did not hear them. She felt as though she was in a dream, and she prayed that she would not be awakened. Nothing seemed real. She had waited so many years for this moment. She willed herself to listen when it came time for the homily.

"The Gospel I have just read was the story of the wedding feast of Cana, the first of Christ's miracles. It was at Cana that marriage was elevated to a sacrament, and it was the first sign given in John's Gospel that the Messianic Age had begun. As prophesized by Isaiah and Amos, the Messianic Age started with the flowing of the choicest wine. How fitting for us to hear this reading at the wedding of someone raised on a vineyard." The congregation laughed, and Marta looked at her son and smiled.

"But what is just as important as the miracles and signs is that a wedding took place, the uniting of two as one, the forging of souls as intended by God from the time of creation. I am honored to be here to celebrate this union and to stand as a witness as Dominic and Marta marry each other. For it is not the priest or the deacon or the minister who marries the bride and groom. We do not make the vows or exchange the rings. It is the couple who marries each other, and nothing could be more fitting than that—for Dominic and Marta, before God and man, friends and family, to declare their love for and pledge themselves to each other in an act of self-sacrifice, of giving of oneself wholly and completely to one another. For their entire lives have been lives of sacrifice."

As Father Sebastian continued, Marta learned even more about Dominic. Aside from a doctor, a lawyer, and several chefs in and around the city, he and his team had helped produce an entrepreneur, several nurses, an anesthesiologist, more than one politician, and even two priests. Monsignor Sebastian extolled Dominic's virtues while also having fun at Dominic's expense. His stories were heart-warming, funny, and in some cases, shocking. It seemed there was nothing Dominic would not do and had not done for his boys, and his dear friend was happy to share all of the escapades, good and bad, with the congregation.

"Dominic has been loved by many throughout his life, and he has touched countless souls, but today we are gathered to see the uniting of just two souls, the joining of two who have waited almost an entire lifetime to finally profess their vows to one another. I first met Dominic shortly after he and Marta said goodbye. I felt his heartache, witnessed his tears, and watched as he battled depression, anger, resentment, and fear. Then I was blessed to watch as he grew from an angry boy into a man of God, taking on the work of St. Paul and St.

Dominic, and others doing God's work with human hands. Dominic is no saint, and he'd be the first one to tell you that." Boisterous laughter echoed across the building. "But he listened when he was called by God. He put others' needs before his own, and he led with his heart. After years of putting others first, of denying himself, and of loving his fellow man unconditionally, the love of God himself, it is time for Dominic to be blessed with the same kind of love. For it was not just Dominic who sacrificed to reach this day. Marta also put others first, including Dominic, when she returned to Italy. They have both sacrificed and loved and lived their lives according to God's will, and he rejoices with them today."

Marta wiped the tears that streamed down her cheeks, and for the first time, she looked out into the many faces around them. Tears glistened on Antonella's and Alexandra's cheeks, and Nicola wiped his eyes with the back of his hand. She smiled at her son, and he beamed back at her, assuring her that all was well.

When Dominic slipped the ring on her finger, the finger that had been without a ring for only the past three months, Marta felt her heart take flight. She took the other ring and slid it down Dominic's finger, repeating the same words, "With this ring, I thee wed." She held his eyes with hers as they were pronounced man and wife, and she thought she would burst with joy. When their lips fused, she never wanted to feel the pain of their separation.

She went through the rest of the Mass as though watching from above. The music and singing sounded like a choir of angels, and the prayers seemed to be the echoes of the Heavenly Hosts. She took Communion in a trance, feeling the overwhelming love of God, Dominic, and even Piero, and knew that he watched from his eternal resting place, showering his blessings upon them. To have walked in the glow of his love for so many years and to now have the love of this incredible man at her side, was more than she had ever dreamed.

"A toast," Paul said loudly over the clink of silver and china and the ripples of conversation around the room. "To my big brother, Dominic, who I always knew would see this day." Paul winked and gestured toward Marta and Dominic with his glass. "May you both spend many days filled with the happiness you deserve, and may your love be like good wine, aged and perfected by many years."

Glasses were raised and voices shouted, "Saluti!"

Marta and Dominic gazed at each other over their glasses, and Marta knew that Paul's words echoed in Dominic's mind as they did in hers.

Dear Lord, may it be your will that our love ages and becomes perfected over many years.

Though her tears flowed as they clinked glasses and took sips of their robust, red wine, Marta knew that the tears were ones of happiness. No matter how much or how little time they had together, their love had already aged and been perfected. Nothing could take that away from them.

Later that evening, while Marta's family was settling down to sleep in the Little Italy house, across the city, Marta and Dominic climbed the stairs to his bedroom together.

In the faint light of the bedroom that Marta, until that night, had only associated with sickness and death, they found a way to breathe life into each other. When Dominic slowly raised the silk camisole, worn beneath Marta's suit, over her head and dropped it onto the floor, she felt no bashfulness. When Dominic's lips pressed to her skin and trailed down her throat and across her breasts, she felt only warmth and desire. When his gentle hands glided lovingly over the full measure of her body, she felt the longing of thirty-six years fade away in a rush of pleasure.

Their days might be numbered, but this night was theirs. She would cherish every touch, every kiss, every stroke, every caress, every word whispered, and every shudder. Love, aged and perfected, unbottled at last.

Isa giggled and wiggled the little toes that peeked out from beneath the heavy blanket of sand. "You are a sand crab!" Alexandra said with a laugh.

Marta watched her grandchildren play in the sand and thought her heart would burst with joy. Carlos broke loose and ran toward the water, and Nicola chased him, sweeping him up in his arms. Beside her in the beach cabana, Dominic slept peacefully with the gondolier's hat covering his face. Though she missed her best friend already, nothing could take away from the joy she felt sitting on the beach with Dominic and her family, their family now.

The waves rolled in off the great Atlantic and crashed on the shore. The sun shone bright in the vast blue sky, and Marta could see far off onto the horizon. Though their honeymoon wasn't traditional in any sense, it was exactly what they both wanted. Dominic wanted to get to know Nicola and the children, and Marta wanted them all to have time together as a family. She refused to think that this might be the only opportunity for them to do that. Sally and Millie's large condo gave them the togetherness as well as the privacy they craved.

Dominic would need to be back in Baltimore the following Monday for his next treatment, but his last one had gone well despite a few days with fever and dizziness. They both hoped that he would continue to battle this illness the way he had battled his way through all the obstacles that life had thrown in his path—with strength and vigor. Knowing that they were in the fight together made the battle easier, or so she thought. Then again, Marta wasn't the one having an IV inserted into her arm every month nor suffering the physical side effects of the drugs.

She looked down at her husband and smiled. Leaving him behind when they were younger had changed her. It had made her stronger, more of a fighter, not someone willing to give up easily or be told what to do. While she readily admitted that their separation had been for the best, she had transferred her hurt and anger into the goal of making her marriage, her vocation as a wife and mother, her very life always count for something. It was that objective that caused her to apply for a job at Il Uffizi so soon after Piero's death and that same drive that propelled her to travel back to the States when the opportunity arose. She would face Dominic's illness with the same intensity and determination that would make their marriage strong and solid and happy.

"Mamma, did you come to the beach when you were little?" she heard Isa ask Alexandra in Italian.

"No, sweetie, I lived far from the beach. We did have lakes that we went to, but not a big ocean like this."

"Like Molveno?"

"Si, much like Lake Molveno."

"That little girl loves to talk," a sleepy Dominic said, stirring and lifting his head and shoulders to smile at Isa. The hat fell onto the sandy blanket beside him.

"Si, she does. Did she wake you?"

"No, not at all. Besides, it feels good to awaken to the sound of little ones. It's not something I've ever had the pleasure of doing before." Marta frowned, but

Dominic continued before her guilt settled in. "What's she talking about?"

"She's asking her mamma if she ever came to the ocean, but Alexandra grew up in Chicago. They're now discussing the similarities between our Italian lakes and the ones near Alexandra's home in the Mid-West."

"I'd forgotten she wasn't from Baltimore. She went to college here. Are her parents still in Chicago?"

"Her mother is. Her father was killed in an accident when she was younger."

"Oh, yes, I think I knew that."

"They're making a short trip to see her mother before they head back home. I'm sure Alexandra would like to stay longer, but the vineyard calls."

"Do they always speak in Italian? That must be difficult for Alex, though she seems to have picked it up pretty well."

"Remarkably well," Marta agreed. "She didn't know a word of Italian when she first arrived. At home they speak both English and Italian. Alexandra is very good about teaching them the words for everything, or as much as possible, in both languages. If any of the children have a desire to take over the vineyard someday, and Nicola prays they will, they must be fluent in many languages. They do many tours now, at Alexandra's insistence, and they must be able to communicate with their visitors and with their buyers around the world."

She and Dominic watched as Isa continued to pepper her mother with questions. "It sounds like a song, the rhythmical cadence of her language, your language. I think I'd like to learn it. My nonna only spoke Italian, and I knew it well as a child, but I'm afraid I lost most of it. Paul could give Isa a run for her money though, in language and number of spoken words."

Marta laughed. "I think you're right. It's no wonder Isa and his granddaughter got along so well at the wedding."

"Two peas in a pod. I hope they can find a way to stay in touch as they get older." His voice was wistful as he gazed out at the horizon.

"They will, Dominic. They have it much easier than we did, and they're family now." They watched Alexandra try to keep up with Isa as she ran to the water and plunged in, washing away the sand that covered her little body. "Angela and I managed for a while, but I let our friendship falter. That was the only sadness I felt on our wedding day. I love Antonella and was so happy that she came and was my maid of honor, something I had not planned on at all, but Angela should have been the one standing by my side. Your cousin, and now mine."

Dominic reached up and took her hand. "She was, mio amore, I know she was." He kissed her knuckles, and she knew he was right.

"Carlos is as red as the grapes in the south field," Nicola said, reaching for a beach towel with which to dry off and wrap up his son.

"And I'm starving," Alexandra said, waddling up the beach, holding her stomach.

"You are always wanting to eat these days," Nicola teased, his eyes full of love for his wife and the child to come.

"I guess it's time to pack up and head back to the condo," Dominic said. "Sally stocked it with enough food for an army, and I'm with Alex. I'm ready to eat."

Marta wondered if he was really hungry or trying to prolong the good vibes from the morning on the beach before the children were beset with grogginess and the pull of afternoon naps. He ate very little these days, and she worried that she would awake one morning and find that he had disappeared in the night, his flesh and bones withering away into nothingness. Rather than allow her good mood to plummet into unwelcome thoughts, she smiled and began packing up, entertaining them with tales of Nicola's childhood visits to the Amalfi Coast.

"He always frightened his father to death," she told them. "We could not keep him away from the water."

Gone was the discomfort of talking about Piero in front of Dominic. On the contrary, he seemed to love hearing about life in Florence, their family adventures, the vineyard, and all the details about her life without him. It made her love him even more.

"Come on, Dominic," she said as the last of their gear was loaded into the beach cart that Sally kept at the beachfront condo. "Let's go feed our family."

Chapter Thirteen

Marta paused to run her hand along the mantle above the fireplace in the living room of the Little Italy house. She straightened the photos aligned there of Zio Roberto and Zia Isabella, Nicola and Alexandra, and now her and Dominic. She threw the last sheet onto a cushioned chair and stood back to make sure she had done everything on her checklist. The children needed to decide what they were going to do with the house. Alexandra wanted to keep it, to have it as a place where they could stay if they came back to the States. It was a terrible expense to keep it up, to have someone check on it and keep it clean throughout the year, yet she understood Alexandra's hesitation to let it go. It tied her to her homeland, to the last place she was Alex O'Donnell, and to the life she once lived. When she first inherited the house, Alex was alone in the world, but having reunited with her mother and marrying Nicola, she was free to let go of the house, but letting go of the past was not easy. Marta knew this well. She had lived it for thirty-six years, and she felt that she was living it again in a new and different way.

She was living at Dominic's house now, *our house*, she had to keep reminding herself. It didn't quite seem real yet, and she wasn't sure how she felt about it—living in someone else's house. Even when Piero bought their first house while she was in America, they moved into it together—their home from day one. Their second home, her apartment in Florence, was still there, still waiting for her to return, much as this house was for Alex. For now, though, her home was with Dominic, and his house was indeed their house. It was going to take some getting used to. The house and the marriage.

She thought about that as she continued her walk through the house. For almost forty years, she was Marta Giordano, almost twice as long as she had been Marta Abelli. For over thirty years, she was Piero's wife. It wasn't as though she didn't remain Marta Abelli, a woman of her own making, not with her education and the job she had at two different points in her life at Il Uffizi. She'd never felt that she had to identify as someone's wife, but still, it was there, a part of her, a large part of whom she was.

An oval mirror hung over the buffet in the dining room, and she stopped to peer at the image. Staring back at her was a woman with long dark hair pulled back into a chignon, much like her aunt had worn hers, dark brown eyes, olive skin that showed how she had spent years protecting and moisturizing it, and a trim, supple body despite her age and aversion to exercise. She'd never had much need for exercise. She grew up running through fields and then lived in a city where cars were unnecessary.

Who are you? Where has this road led you? What are you meant to be doing now?

She had no problem being Dominic's wife, but she had always been more than that. Once she hit adulthood, she was always doing something other than maintaining a marriage and a home. She worked at the museum, she took pictures, she dabbled with painting despite knowing that she really had no talent for it. She raised a child, volunteered at her church and in her community, and though she shared no parts of the business, she was always there when Nicola needed advice about the vineyard. Now, she had no job as she had formally quit hers, no child to take care of anymore, no art studio, and nothing to photograph.

Suddenly, an idea began to take shape, like a specter rising from the grave, floating, waving, forming itself into a recognizable shape. Could she do it? What would her husband say? What would he think? How would he feel?

She raced up the stairs to her bedroom, her former bedroom, and pulled out the envelope that she had tucked away in the top drawer of the dresser. She carefully removed the photo of young a Dominic and gazed at his radiant smile, his Mediterranean blue eyes, and the dimples, so deep she could almost put her finger into them.

She thought about the photographs she had taken of Dominic and the boys after the basketball game, and the ones she had taken of him on her phone by the docks, in his office, on the beach, wherever it struck her that this was a moment she wanted to remember.

She thought about Monsignor Sebastian's homily at their wedding, the stories he told, the things he said about her husband. She recalled the stories she'd heard from Paul, Sally, and the young men at the center. Paul's comparison of his brother to St. Dominic came to mind as well.

She reached back into the drawer and removed the leather-bound journal, long abandoned but never forgotten. She ran her finger along the spine and opened the book. She read the last words that she had written in it, the same words that ended the letter she had written to Dominic on that fateful day so long ago.

You are good, Dominic. You are worthy. You will be a great man someday, and I will count the days, even if they number the stars, until I can once again look into your eyes.

I will be forever yours.

Marta

The more she thought about it, the more the idea took hold, and the specter became real, a living, growing being that could not be put back. This was something she realized she needed to do, but how should she approach Dominic, and would he agree?

Dominic watched her with wary eyes, his head propped on a pillow. He looked so tired, so weak, and she suddenly worried that her idea was too much for him, would cost him too much. He was so humble, so careful not to take credit for all that he had done. He shied away from all interviews, from photographs, even from accepting well-deserved awards. She stopped talking and reached out to touch his face. She gently rubbed the back of her fingers on his stubbly chin.

"It is too much. I am sorry. I should not have brought it up."

She tried to smile and took her hand away, but he caught it in his own, his reflexes still as inexplicably good as ever.

"Maybe it's time. The center will need to keep going. They'll need ways to sustain it once I'm not here to milk my network." He gave her a wry smile, and though his words pained her, she did not comment. They had both come to accept that the time would be here soon for the center to go on without him. "I know someone. She'd like to hear about this. I'll call her."

Marta chuckled, "Of course, you do. You know someone everywhere who can help with whatever you want or need. That does not surprise me. But this idea, this project of mine, it is all right? You do not mind?"

This time, Dominic reached out and held her chin in his hand like he had done so many times before. He looked into her eyes, and she saw the depths of his love.

"It won't be easy. Already, there are days I don't want you or anybody else to see me. There'll be more days when I won't like the way I look or act or feel. But it's your love that has brought me through my darkest hours, through my despair, through times I lacked faith or the will to live. Who am I to deny you this request? But please, remember one thing."

"What is it, cara?"

"There is only one St. Dominic who did the work I do, and he is not me."

"You do not have to be saint for the world to know your name and all that you have done. You are an inspiration to so many. Let me share your story, please."

"How can I refuse you anything? I love you with all my being, and I will give you anything in my power."

She smiled, closed her eyes, and leaned into his touch. She felt him sit up and move closer to her, sensed his nearness, and tingled with anticipation as she leaned down so that his lips caressed hers, gently at first and then with more hunger.

"Let's leave the talk and the planning until later," he whispered against her cheek.

She let him take her hand and pull her down onto the bed beside him. Their lovemaking was slow and gentle, and she savored every kiss, every touch, and every moment God gave them to be together.

Though Dominic was told that the medications and chemotherapy would most likely impede his abilities to make love to her, he proved the doctors wrong. That was no surprise to Marta. She had witnessed his steel will and resolve, but more than that, she knew the power of their love for each other. It had survived forces stronger than any disease.

Marta spent weeks going through photographs that Paul gave to her. She carefully selected the right ones, catalogued them, and made notes about them. She looked for hours at Dominic's face, his eyes, his expression that hid nothing, and she recognized his thoughts and his feelings in each pose. She smiled and frowned and laughed and cried. There was so much of his life that she had missed, so much that she still knew nothing about, yet he was still here, still able to fill in the gaps, still able to help her put together the pieces of the enormous puzzle.

Dominic didn't deny her when she asked if she could take pictures, not on his best days nor on his worst. The rawness of the photographs sometimes pained her, but she continued on. For the first time since that summer, she wrote, journaling all of her feelings and writing down his, often dictated to her late at night in the privacy of their bedroom, their naked bodies tangled together, where they had no inhibitions of any kind. That love and trust showed in her writing and in the photographs she took.

After their first meeting with Melissa West, Marta had a well laid-out plan and a promise from an agent to look at her finished work. Melissa was a photojournalist who grew up in Baltimore but now lived on Maryland's Eastern Shore with her husband and children. She had published many books of her photographs as well as a best-selling book about her years on the run and how she managed to stay alive while being pursued by a killer. Melissa's mother had gone to school with Dominic, and they were friends even through his dark years. He had grieved her death and then followed the story of Melissa's disappearance and the accusations cast upon her. Once she resurfaced, safe and well, Dominic had reached out, and they remained in touch, discovering only recently that Melissa's murdered friend was Alex's brother. It certainly was a small world.

Marta had been transfixed by the young woman and her story but realized that their stories were not so different. They both faced impossible choices and did what they needed to do to make lives for themselves. They both fought back and took their fates into their own hands after the actions of others dictated the directions of their lives, and eventually they both found immeasurable love and happiness. Most of all, they both trusted in God's plan for their lives.

Following Melissa's advice, Marta began assembling her photographs and writing, creating a work of art more beautiful and more powerful than she had even dreamed.

By the time Marta said goodbye to Little Italy, to America, to Dominic's family, and to the two lives she had lived there, she was ready to put the final touches on her artistic masterpiece. She had been blessed in many ways, and she would never forget the gifts God had given to her, especially the gift of Dominic's love and the time they had together. She headed back to Italy with a heart full of love.

Two Years Later

Marta walked through the fields with her hand outstretched to touch the feathery leaves that opened to the sun. She inhaled the intoxicating scent of the grapes that surrounded her and knew that it had been the right decision to come here. She craved the peace and quiet that the vineyard offered, but even more, she craved the love and support of her family. Paul and Sophia, Sally and Millie, and all of the young men at the center had become family, of course, but the city was too big, too loud, and too dirty. Even Florence could not offer what was needed now. This, Belle Uve, was the right place to go, the right place to be, and the right place to stay. It was home.

She stopped and turned her face up toward the sun, letting the heat and light wash over her. This was another new beginning, another fresh start. She felt as though she had led so many lives—little girl, daughter, niece, young woman in love with two men, wife, mother, working woman, grandmother, and then nurse. The last had been the most exhausting and the most fulfilling, next to mother and grandmother. Some days, particularly near the end of the treatments, it had taken all she could possibly give to remain standing and smiling until she collapsed into bed that night, the man that she loved by her side.

And how she loved him. She had spent every minute of that trying time showing him, telling him, always reassuring him that she loved him. Even on the days— no, especially on the days—he urged her to leave him, to return to Italy, to give him the dignity of not dying in front of her, caring for him was never too much, never too hard, never a chore or a bother. As she'd been taught as a child, she offered all of the work and all of the pain up as prayer. She prayed constantly. She prayed for strength. She prayed for guidance. She prayed that he would be comforted, that his pain would be eased, that he would be cured…

"Marta!"

She turned toward the voice and was struck by the brilliance of his smile which surpassed the luminosity of the sun itself.

"You found me," she said, walking toward him.

He took her in his arms and kissed her, his dark, wavy hair brushing her forehead as his strong arms held her tightly. When he released her, she looked up into those beautiful eyes the color of the sea.

"Didn't I promise you that I would? I found you when I could not keep you, and then I found you again just when I thought all was lost, and yet I keep finding you again and again. You thought you would lose me, but I will never stop finding you."

"It's still so hard to believe. I was just thinking about it all and what a miracle it is that we are here, that you are here. I thank God every day that you are well and that he has given us another day together."

"You are my miracle, my gift from God. I knew it the day I first saw you. You saved me then, and you saved me two years ago when you came back into my life. How could I not be well? God brought you to me so I could have a reason to fight, a reason to live. When I was resigned to leave this world, he sent you as a reminder that I needed to have faith, to remember that all things are possible with God."

"You didn't need me to remind you of that." She shook her head and smiled. "Your faith alone is more than enough to move mountains."

"My faith is what compelled me to always believe that you would return to me, and it was what tells me that you and I are not done yet."

After a passionate kiss, Marta took his hand and led him down the row. Broad, green leaves waved in the breeze, and they could hear the laughter of Isa, Carlos, and little Pablo from somewhere nearby until they'd walked far enough that the drone of saws and hammering of nails drowned out the sounds of the children's play. Marta wondered sometimes if the children were painful reminders of the life he left behind, but he assured her that his heart only had room for love and happiness and not sorrow or pain.

Dominic would always play an important role in the work and operation of the Seton Center, but he had a new project to oversee now. The house was coming together nicely, a smaller version of the villa where Marta had grown up that was Nicola and Alexandra's home now.

Dominic's doctor recommended that he leave the city and spend the rest of his life—years if it was God's will—breathing in fresh air and allowing his lungs to heal and rehabilitate. As far as Marta knew, there was no better place for that to happen than here. This was the land where her father had healed from the mental trauma of war and where Zio Roberto healed from the physical trauma. It was where she had healed after returning from America while preparing for her wedding to Piero. It was where Alexandra had healed after losing so many she loved, and it was where Nicola had healed after he fell from the roof, when he came to know that he was in love with Alexandra.

Marta recalled the passages in scripture when God referred to the Promised Land as a vineyard, the place where his people would finally be at home and where the choicest wine flowed. She smiled at the thought. As a little girl and teenager, she had counted the days until she could leave this place. She had fled to America, seeking greener pastures, only to have her heart broken. In marriage, she had embraced living in Florence, but she always cherished her visits to the villa that her younger self couldn't wait to leave.

St. Paul taught that in God's vineyard, there is no anxiety, only thanksgiving and peace. That's just what she felt now, standing with her hand in Dominic's, watching *their* house being built.

"Nonna e Nonno! Come! It is here!"

They turned toward Isa's voice. She was running down the row toward them, her dark hair flowing behind her.

"Papà says to come. You have to be the one to open the box." She turned back and ran toward the house, and they hurried after her. Marta's heart raced but not from the rush to the house.

She held her breath as she tore the packing tape and reached into the box. With trembling hands, she lifted the top book and ran her fingers lightly across the cover. A twenty-two-year-old Dominic looked up at her, his sea blue eyes sparkling with laughter. The story of his life— the mistake that changed its course, their meeting and parting, the opening of the center, all of his work with the boys and all of the deeds for his community that had been kept secret for so long, his diagnosis, their reunion, and his fight to live—was carefully documented in words and in pictures.

Marta gently opened the book and scrolled through the pages, stopping in the center to slowly flip through the pictures that detailed his life and his brush with death.

She looked at Dominic and saw tears that matched her own. She closed the book and ran her finger along the title, one they had chosen together.

"All Things Are Possible," she read, echoing the words Dominic had spoken just moments before.

"With you and with God, they are." His words were low, his voice strained with emotion.

"Let us celebrate," Nicola said. "We will open a bottle of the good wine."

They all worked together to move the boxes of books into the office where Alexandra and Maria would fill the shelves that awaited their arrival, and then they retreated to the villa where they toasted each other with the finest wine the vineyard had to offer.

Inscription from *All Things Are Possible*
By Marta Abelli Giordano D'Angelo

Dear Reader,

Alfred Lord Tennyson wrote that "It is better to have loved and lost than to never have loved at all." I say that it is better to have loved and lost twice than to never have loved either one. The story in the book before you is one of bad choices, hardships, surrender, and rebirth, a story of heroism and quiet triumph, but it is first and foremost a story of love. It is the story of people who loved each other enough to sacrifice all that they had and all that they were in order to do what was best for each other. It is also the story of how love reaches beyond years and geography and even science and finds, touches, and heals. It is a story that shows how taking the harder road is often the path on which God blesses us abundantly.

I have always loved the reading from St. John about the wedding feast at Cana. The steward, after drinking the water turned into wine exclaims, "Everyone serves good wine first, and then when people have drunk freely, an inferior one; but you have kept the good wine until now."

A skilled vintner knows from the start that a particular crop will be good, perhaps the best, and that the wine will be special, and he keeps that wine in the barrel for many years before bottling it. He ages and perfects that wine until he knows it is the good wine that he has patiently waited for.

Since the day I first left my family's vineyard in Italy to head to America, I have grown older and wiser. I was blessed to have loved not one but two wonderful men. Neither was superior or inferior, but my heart has learned that love is something that grows over time and like wine, ages and perfects. That was true for me and my husband, Piero, and it was true for me and my first and last true love, Dominic. Our love became bolder, fuller, and better over time.

I have lived through many of life's ceremonies, the rites and rituals, the sacrifices, the feasts, and the toasts. For whatever time I have left on this earth, I will love and appreciate all that God has given to me, especially whatever time I have left with Dominic. I will spend the rest of my life drinking the good wine.

May God bless you and the road you choose.

Marta

About the Author

Amy began writing as a child and never stopped. She wrote articles for magazines and newspapers before writing children's books and adult fiction. A graduate of the University of Maryland with a Master of Library and Information Science, Amy worked as a librarian for fifteen years and, in 2010, began writing full time.

Amy now writes inspirational women's fiction for people of all ages. She has published two children's books and numerous novels, including the award-winning novels *Picture Me*, *Whispering Vines*, and the Chincoteague Island Trilogy. A former librarian, Amy enjoys a busy life on the Eastern Shore of Maryland.

The recipient of numerous national literary awards, including the Illumination Award, LYRA award, Independent Publisher Book Award, International Digital Award, and the Golden Quill Award as well as honors from the Catholic Press Association and the Eric Hoffer Book Award, Amy's writing has been hailed "a verbal masterpiece of art" (author Alexa Jacobs) and "Everything you want in a book" (Amazon reviewer). Amy's books are available internationally, wherever books are sold, in print and eBook formats.

Follow Amy at:
http://amyschislerauthor.com
http://facebook.com/amyschislerauthor
https://twitter.com/AmySchislerAuth
https://www.goodreads.com/amyschisler

Book Club Discussion Questions

1. Though Marta was engaged to Piero when she first arrived in America, she soon discovered that her "love" for him was not as strong as what she felt for Dominic. She questioned which one was really love, which feelings were actually real. What do you think? Did she really love Piero, or did her heart belong to Dominic. Is it possible that she was right in saying she loved them both?

2. Marta kept the truth about Piero, that he was her fiancé, from Dominic, and she kept the truth about loving Dominic from Piero. Was she right or wrong in either case? Was she justified in not being honest with them? Can something be deceitful without being sinful?

3. When young Marta left America, she told herself that it was for the best, that she was leaving for Dominic's sake. Do you believe that? Do you think that her leaving was selfish or selfless?

4. For thirty-six years, Marta kept her romance with Dominic a secret, believing that she was doing so for all the right reasons. Have you ever kept a secret for many years for the right reasons? Did you ever divulge it to anyone? What were the consequences of keeping the secret and then divulging it?

5. Dominic attributes his success in life to God and to following God's plan. Do you see areas in your own life

where you achieved success because you followed God's plan for you?

6. They say it takes a village to raise a family. In Dominic's case, it takes a village to bring him out of his depression and to give him purpose and then an entire city to continue the success of the Seton Center. Have you ever been a part of a village that helped someone or something succeed? How did that make you feel? How important is the building of a village to the building of a person or an entity?

7. Marta is worried about how Nicola will take the news of his mother dating someone new after the death of his father. Have you ever been in Marta's situation? In Nicola's? How did you feel, and how did you handle it?

8. Marta, even as young woman, recognized that part of her attraction to Dominic was his resemblance to her father. As an adult and mother, she saw some of those qualities in her son. Do you think we are attracted to people who exhibit the same characteristics as those we love, both good and bad? Do you see similar attributes between your husband and father, wife and mother, sibling and friend?

9. What role do you believe Paul played in the book? Did he help or hinder the relationship between Marta and Dominic. Do you think that one truly was the good brother and the other was the bad brother?

10. When Marta and Dominic celebrate their wedding night, she feels no embarrassment or inhibitions. Do you think this is because she has always thought of Dominic as being a part of her, or do you think it's the wisdom of her age and maturity, or perhaps the knowledge and acceptance that neither of their bodies is perfect? If you were Antonella, and Marta were to ask you advice about her wedding night, what would you tell her?

11. There have been tremendous strides made in the treatment and curing of cancer over the last fifty years. Even advanced cancer is not always a death sentence. Do you know someone who fought the odds and lived? Did that change their perspective on life? If so, how?

12. How does the title fit the book?